THE DINOSAUR BATTLE OF NEW ORLEANS
VELOCIRAPTORS IN THE VIEUX CARRÉ

DANE HATCHELL

SEVERED PRESS
HOBART TASMANIA

THE DINOSAUR BATTLE OF NEW ORLEANS

PROLOGUE

Captain Thomas Wesselman was an angel descending from Heaven as he piloted the 737 toward its destination. The sky was an ocean of blue, without a hint of a cloud as far as the eye could see. Landings and takeoffs were the only times now that he truly felt alive. Life was so different during his time in Desert Storm, when he flew an A-10 Warthog. Wesselman had thirty missions to his credit and took out multiple tanks, APCs, SAM sites, and radar installations.

Those days were long gone. The warrior inside the military man had never died, but Wesselman had to make compromises in civilian life. He was nearing twenty years as a commercial pilot, with the Grim Reaper of retirement looming before him with its deadly scythe ready to clip his wings.

"We are about to catch the localizer. Our speed has to be below two hundred and fifty knots and our angle less than thirty degrees," Wesselman said to his co-pilot. "Can you tell me if it's time to engage the autopilot?"

First officer Jim Hall quickly scanned the gauges, and said, "Roger that. But you have to get permission to descend to three thousand feet first."

"Good for you. I tried to hurry you along to see if you'd forget. You passed the test," Wesselman said. "Go ahead and make the call."

"Yes sir." Hall grabbed the mic and pushed the button. "New Orleans, Delta two-thirty-six will be descending to three thousand feet for runway twenty-two."

The radio squawked back, "Delta two-thirty-six, you have an all-clear on runway twenty-two."

Wesselman took the mic from Hall. "How're the hurricanes down there?"

1

"Hurricanes? Nothing but blue bird skies over here," the control tower said.

"I'm talking about the drinks at Pat O'Leary's in the French Quarter. *New Orleans* is the only city in the world to have hurricanes year round."

"Ha-ha, Delta two-thirty-six. Hurricanes at Pat O's are always Cat-Five!" the control tower said. "In fact…"

Dead silence filled the cabin as the transmission stopped for an uncomfortably long time.

Wesselman shot his gaze over to Hall, who had raised eyebrows turned his way and a growing look of concern on his face.

The radio came back to life, "Request denied, Delta two-thirty-six. Level out and prepare to ascend to twenty thousand."

The sudden change in the controller's orders and demeanor snapped Wesselman to attention. He had learned a long time ago questioning orders in an emergency often led to immediate doom. "Roger, MSY. Leveling out and heading to twenty thousand."

"I wonder what's going on down there," Hall said.

"Could be a few things. Another aircraft may have a problem and needs to land first. The controller might have realized they assigned the runaway to two different planes. Happens more times than it should. And," Wesselman sank back in his chair as the plane leveled out, "in this day and time, there might be a bomb threat or a terrorist attack on the airport."

"I'll plot a course for Lakefront Airport, just in case they close MSY down," Hall said. "You better inform the passengers so they won't get spooked."

The radio sparked to life again, "Delta two-thirty-six, radar just picked up unknowns at your altitude. Any visuals?"

*

Mark Chaney drank his third cup of coffee and loaded his bottom lip with the second dip of the day. He had enjoyed smokeless tobacco since the age of eight, where the nicotine kept him alert for early morning hunts on his uncle's property. His system had hardened enough that he could dip and drink coffee, or any other beverage, for that matter. There was no need to spit, as

Mark learned over the years how to slowly ingest the *juice*. Ten years of long hours as an air traffic controller made dipping tobacco a necessity, not a luxury.

His gaze fixed on the radar, Mark paid extra attention to the screen as always with arrivals and departures. When the anomalous blip suddenly appeared near a descending jet, he first thought he had a broken monitor. Objects didn't just materialize out of thin air, especially this size and this high in the air. But a redundant radar screen showed the same irregularity.

"Ritchie," Mark called out to his supervisor. "We've got a problem over here."

Ritchie Lamoine had just given Delta 236 permission to drop to three thousand feet. He removed his headset and quickly stepped over to Mark's side.

Hovering behind Mark's back, Ritchie said, "What the heck is that?"

"Sorta looks like birds, but not really. They're too big," Mark said.

Heading for the tower window, Ritchie snatched a pair of binoculars from his desk and searched the sky.

"See anything?" Mark asked.

The binoculars came down, and Ritchie wiped his eyes, a scowl had hold of his face. The binoculars went back up, and he said, "Holy heck."

"What is it?"

"It's not birds."

"Drones? I've been afraid of a drone attack for a long time now." Mark strained from his seat to get a visual through the window with no luck.

"You're not going to believe it," Ritchie said. "*I* don't believe it."

"Good god, man. What is it?" Mark was on his feet, fear weakening his knees.

"*Pterodactyls*."

CHAPTER 1

Earlier that day:

Bridget Reed leisurely drove along Feret Street in her red Mustang, feeling the onset of indigestion from chowing down the last half of her duck sausage roll from Dat Dog. It was Saturday, and she had planned to spend the day shopping on Magazine Street for some new fall clothes. As her luck went, her phone rang, interrupting lunch.

The call was from the Tulane University—School of Science and Engineering. Dread washed over her at the thought there might be a problem with the upcoming fall schedule. She specifically enrolled in summer school to ensure her a seat in Computer Science 225: Pseudorandomness. With trepidation, she cleared her throat and answered her phone.

It surprised Bridget to hear the voice of Dr. Bryan Breaux. Dr. Breaux was one of her professors. *Why would he be calling from the university on a Saturday?* They lived in New Orleans, Louisiana. There were more things to do in the *Big Easy* than fifty-two Saturdays could fill. It was time to let the good times roll. *Laissez les bons temps rouler!*

Dr. Breaux's request surprised Bridget even more. He wanted her to come to the science building *now*. At least her school schedule wasn't in jeopardy. Breaux's cryptic call had added a layer of mystery, which didn't help the digesting process of Bridget's stomach with that duck sausage.

What other choice did she have but go? His plea for her to come had been laced with desperation and a twinge of excitement. Diagnosed with pancreatic cancer, the poor man didn't have much longer to live. Bridget didn't understand why the man continued to work. Dr. Breaux should be on a cruise, living it up before that option would be taken off the table.

She slowed and turned onto Engineering Road, looking for a place to park between the science building and the mechanical services building. The choices were many, so she eased next to one of the handicapped spaces and turned off the engine.

Getting out of the car, the four-story, bricked behemoth of a science building sat in front of her. Bridget's destination, though, was behind the building. So, she took the walkway between the mechanical service building and the science building for her final destination.

She had never been to this part of the campus on a Saturday before. As far as Bridget could tell, there was no one else around. It made her feel exposed, vulnerable, and questioning why the heck she didn't trust that little voice in her head that said she should turn and head back to the car.

The sun had the walk between the buildings heating up like an oven. It wasn't until she stepped past the buildings and onto Johnston Quad, where the shade of an old oak tree hid the harsh rays, and allowed her to breathe easier.

Turning left, she saw the temporary building; an eyesore in the otherwise park-like setting of the quad. Tulane University and NASA had a joint venture to study quantum entanglement. Quantum entanglement was a phenomenon where twin particles, separated by distance, mimicked each other. Applying force to one particle affected the other particle the same way. The objective was to advance communication between two points without the use of cables or even radio waves. That would make communications faster and hack-proof.

The University had received a grant, and the two-year project was near completion. Dr. Breaux started the project but didn't give up his duties as a professor. Teaching, he said, had always been his passion.

As Bridget neared the building, the electrical hum from the University's electrical substation rose, sounding like cicadas on a lazy summer afternoon. They placed the ugly temporary building in Johnston Quad to access the electrical grid; even though it spoiled the natural tranquility. Once the experimental device proved operational, NASA would disassemble the whole building and its contents, and relocate it somewhere else.

When Bridget reached the door, it was locked tight. *Really*! A card reader to the left blinked red. She thought about knocking on the door, but at this point, a *locked door* seemed like a good enough excuse to leave and salvage a day of shopping.

The door opened before she had a chance to turn and bolt for freedom.

"Bridget! I'm so glad to see you." Dr. Bryan Breaux, his hair slick with oil and glasses slightly crooked on his face, wrapped his arms around her and squeezed.

Bridget's arms hung by her side, taken totally off-guard by the professor's show of emotion.

"I don't know what I would have done if you hadn't come. You're my last hope," Breaux said, sighing loudly as he released her from his embrace.

"Is everything okay, Dr. Breaux? You don't seem like yourself," Bridget said as she took a step back, turning her head to the side and giving him a wary eye.

Dr. Breaux dropped his gaze and took a deep breath. "Bridget, everything is *not* all right. You are aware of my…condition." He paused and bit his lip, then, removed his glasses and wiped his eyes. "God, I feel so selfish right now…" he said as if to himself. "Come inside, please, and I'll explain everything." He pushed the door further open and invited her in.

It wasn't too late to turn and run. Bridget considered, though, the professor's one hundred and fifty pounds hung on his six-foot frame. If anything improper were to occur, she thought she could take him in a fair fight.

Bridget passed through a short hall where two offices resided. Beyond that, the room opened into a large unpartitioned area, NASA's scientific apparatus took up the bulk of the room.

"You're looking at the Quantum Entanglement Device or Q.E.D. Sometimes we refer to it as *Q*. Sometimes we'll call it *Ked* because of the phonetic way to say Q.E.D. I'm sure you're well aware of the interest in quantum entanglement, as a science, and as a potential industry."

"I've read some things about quantum entanglement," Bridget said. "The Chinese currently have the record for distance. They put a satellite in orbit and successively completed an experiment between space and Earth."

"Uncle Sam doesn't want a competing interest to take the lead. Q here has gone through all the simulation routines and is ready for service."

Bridget's right hand waved the air before her. "Okay, great, so why did you call me here?" She realized after she spoke that her tone might have been a bit on the *get on with it* side.

Breaux stared blankly. And then, as if he reached deep inside and found his inner strength, he said, "I called you here to save my life."

"Save your life?" Bridget smirked, her eyes darting side to side. "Dr. Breaux, I'm not sure I can help you there. You have pancreatic cancer. I don't have any medical training. Your best bet is to see the doctors at Ochsner Medical Center down the street, or M.D. Anderson, in Texas."

"No, they can't help me." He turned his head toward the Q.E.D., then pointed to it. "That is my only hope. The Q," he turned back to Bridget, "and you."

"Obviously, Doc, I'm just a sheep grazing in the field. You'll have to explain this to me."

Dr. Breaux raised his hands. "I know. I know. I'm being selfish—getting ahead of myself. But I've worked so hard..." His face contorted in pain as if someone had just shoved a knife into his gut. He shook it off, and said, "Now that the Q is operational, NASA will start on Monday, taking it apart, and shipping it out."

"So?"

"So, I need you to use the Q on me. It's the only shot I have at beating this cancer."

Bridget hadn't a clue how the Q could cure cancer, but there was no doubt Dr. Breaux believed it. Whether the man was of sound mind was another question. "Tell me more."

"NASA redirected their resources toward national defense, now that we don't have much of a manned space program anymore. Bridget, Q is more than just a quantum entanglement device. It also can be used as a *quantum transporting device*."

"Quantum transporting? That's stuff in Star Trek movies," Bridget said, seriously believing the professor's medication needed adjusting.

"Not anymore. I've run all the preliminary tests. Q is ready for service in the quantum entanglement, *and*, quantum transportation service."

"I don't get it. You want me to beam you to another planet or something where they might have a cure for cancer?"

"Nothing that outlandish," Breaux said. "I found out I had pancreatic cancer almost six months ago. Pancreatic cancer is a death sentence. I've avoided all the treatments that may prolong my life, or end it sooner, to work on a cure. A cure I've perfected this morning. That's why I called you. I need you to help me cure my cancer by operating the Q. You'll have to enter the sequences manually. I can't do this alone."

"How is the Q going to cure your cancer?" As wild as the story sounded, Bridget sensed that there might be real hope at this point.

"Q is designed to replicate atom for atom, and in the case of living tissue, cell for cell, in the transportation process. I've created a program that replaces the cancer cells with normal cells. When Q disassembles my cancer-ridden body and then reassembles it, I will be free of cancer."

Bridget's face lit up. "Doc, that's wonderful!" Her smile quickly faded when reality returned. "Wait, how sure are you that this will work?"

"I believe it will work based on the simulation I ran."

"You ran a computer simulation, *great*. Have you successfully transported a living creature?"

"No."

"No?" The answer did take Bridget off-guard.

"The power requirements are massive. Performing an actual test might alert others as to my," Breaux hesitated a moment, "*personal endeavor*."

"So, you don't actually know if the program and Q are safe to use." She thought some more. "What's the worst thing that could happen when I transport you?"

Breaux tilted his head and spread his hands apart. "The worst thing that could happen is that *I could die*."

"And you chose me to have the honor of being the one who kills you?"

"It's not like that at all. Bridget, I'll die soon if it doesn't work. You won't be killing me if something goes wrong." Breaux's lips quivered, and he managed to eke out, "Don't you see? I'm *already dead*." He gasped as he tried to hold his tears back.

How did she come to be in this place? It was Saturday. She was having lunch at Dat Dog and should be shopping right now. Heck, she thought she might go to the French Quarter later tonight and hook up with some friends she knew were going to the Cat's Mcow.

Instead, she had a man dying of cancer asking her to be a part of what may turn out to be an unwitting suicide.

Dr. Breaux was a broken man. She realized he had no good options before him. What if she had cancer and needed the professor's help? Seeing there were no sure answers, she said, "Why me, Dr. Breaux? I'm one of your students, but it's not like we have any personal relationship outside of class. There are probably a hundred other students you could have asked to help. Again, why me?"

"Because of a paper you wrote as a freshman on the *Right to Die*. I know what you went through with your father. I read you fought his decision to undergo assisted suicide until you saw it was the most humane thing to do. You were there with him when he died. Holding his hand...and showing unselfish love. That was the greatest gift you could ever give him."

Tears streamed down Bridget's face. That day would never leave her memory. It was the hardest thing she had ever done in her life, but it was also the most rewarding. Dr. Breaux needed her now just like her dad had needed her then. "Show me what to do, Dr. Breaux. Even if this becomes your last wish in life, I want to help give you that chance."

The tension gripping the professor's cheeks melted. "Thank you...I was counting on your understanding. I don't know..." He stopped speaking, and then with his eyebrows reaching for his hairline, he said, "I'm ready. Let's do this!"

Dr. Breaux headed toward the Q. The bulk of the apparatus was rectangular shaped, with one end morphing into a tube resembling the barrel of an alien cannon. Opposite of the tube side, a small desk with two computers operated as the control center.

Bridget followed behind and watched as he called the two computer screens to life.

"Okay, so the computer on the left is tied into the electrical grid. It takes a lot of power for the entanglement experiments. To use Q for transporting, it takes even more. So, I had to hack into the regional power grid and divert electricity to our substation," Breaux said. "Do you remember a couple of months ago when we had that bad rain and Lakefront, the French Quarter, and other areas flooded because of the water pumps in the pumping stations didn't work?"

"Sure, the mayor took a lot of heat over that."

"Well, it wasn't Mitch Edwards' fault. He blamed the Sewerage and Water Board, and they blamed the power company. Those pumping stations didn't have power because of me."

"Why did you do that?" Bridget asked.

"The program is designed to put a load on electrical substations with excess capacity. Most of those substations include the pumps. Unfortunately, there was a glitch in the program that shifted loads across the power grid, cutting off power to a good number of pumps. The bad part of it all, I didn't know how to *un-do* the error. It took me a couple of days to find the problem and fix it. By that time, the power company found ways to bypass my interference and set the grid straight."

"It's a good thing it hasn't rained in two weeks. A lot of people flooded during that storm."

"Bridget, I've beat myself up over it ever since. At this point, all I can do is say *I'm sorry* in my heart and say a prayer for forgiveness. But I've come this far, and I intend to see it to the end. The transportation process will take less than a minute. Interruption of services on the power grid will be minimal."

"The computer on the left is flashing *START*. All I have to do is click on that icon, and it'll redirect the power?" Bridget asked.

"Correct. Then, the computer on the right, you'll have three different prompts that will begin and complete the transporting process."

"Where will you be transported to?"

"Ah, yes," Breaux said and nodded. "I considered testing distance for the first experiment but decided not to push my luck. I set the machine to move me backward one millimeter. So, it won't appear as if I've moved at all."

"You said there were three prompts. What should I expect at each?"

"After engaging the first, Q will send a positronic beam that will measure and record *the spin* direction of every particle in my body. The second will change the organic components in my body into energy. The third takes the recorded information of my cells, with the patch I put in that will convert my cancer cells to normal cells, and reassemble me back together good as new."

Bridget closed her left eye, and her lips scrunched together like she had eaten something sour. "You make it sound so simple, but I know if you really broke it down it would sound dangerous."

"You're right. I did leave the worst part out."

"The worst part? You mean how every cell in your body might cook like fried chicken?"

"No, the part where I have to take off my clothes before we do this."

"I've got to see your skinny, white ass naked? I'll pass."

"Where I'll be standing, Q will block your view from the waist down. You're safe."

"Okay, I'm back in." Bridget sighed, and her shoulders slumped. "Dr. Breaux, I don't mean to be making light of the situation, but I do that when I'm nervous. Seriously, what if your body catches on fire or Q turns you into a heaping mass of organic material? I'll have to call the police, and they'll blame me for your murder."

"I've thought about that. I've set up an email to send an hour from now where I explain that I set all of this up on my own and take sole responsibility. I'll delete that email if all goes well. If the worst happens, you can tell the authorities I called you right before the experiment, and you came to check on me. The phone records will prove that's true. If I die, you can call the police and simply say you found me dead."

"Since you *are* risking your life, it does seem like you've thought this through," Bridget said, knowing arguing another point wouldn't change the professor's mind. With a deep breath and setting her shoulder blades straight, she said, "Okay, I'm ready."

Breaux's eyes widened in excitement. "Thank you. I've made my peace with God, and there's no reason to continue the suspense." He stepped over to the computer on the left side and set the program running. Without saying another word, he bolted over near Q's barrel and began undressing.

Bridget hovered behind the two computers and watched the hack divert electricity between substations. As each sequence completed, the electrical hum from the breakers outside increased.

Naked, Breaux took his spot in front of Q.

It pained Bridget to look at him. Clothing had hidden the emaciation of his body as cancer robbed nutrients from muscle to feed its voracious appetite. The sad sight hardened her resolve to carry through. If the experiment killed the professor, she would consider it an act of mercy and not murder.

The breakers outside screamed with overload. The power hack program registered *complete*.

"It's ready, Dr. Breaux," Bridget hollered over the noise.

His chest swole with a deep breath of fresh air. "Begin positron mapping."

The sequence started, Q woke like a ferocious animal, deeply growling, and threatening anyone in its path.

Dr. Breaux seemed to freeze in time. Unable to move and oblivious to anything around him.

Bridget's insides shook; feeling the energy of the powerful machine in her bones. If she could have moved her legs, she might have run.

The computer screen showed the first sequence complete.

With her heart in her throat, Bridget started the second sequence.

Q's cry shifted to a frequency so low the floor shook.

Dr. Breux's body faded as if it had turned into air.

The noise in the lab was such that Bridget didn't hear herself as she screamed. Waves of energy surged throughout the room as if she experienced the power of elemental creation.

The second sequence had completed.

She quickly started the third sequence, damning all fear of the abominable machine.

Seconds ticked away like hours. At the crescendo of chaos, right when Bridget worried she'd breached the wall of sanity, Q's roar morphed into a soft moan.

At this point, she realized her eyes were tightly shut. She slowly opened them and saw the power hack had reversed its sequence.

Bridget looked up in time to see Dr. Breaux standing as he was in the beginning, right before he collapsed to the floor.

"Dr. Breaux!" Bounding around the desk, she hurried over to his unmoving body.

Breaux's eyes blinked as Bridget knelt by his side. "Dr. Breaux? Can you hear me?" She grabbed his hand and patted it. "Dr. Breaux?

His head turned toward her. He stopped blinking and focused on her face.

"Dr. Breaux? Are you okay?"

Opening his mouth, moving the stiffness out of his lips, he said, "Bridget, I've been on the most amazing journey."

CHAPTER 2

"Pterodactyls? Are you nuts?" Mark Chaney, the air traffic controller, yelled in disbelief. His eyes wide and bottom teeth framed in dark tobacco.

Ritchie Lemoine dashed over to the radio and grabbed the handset. "Delta two-thirty-six, radar just picked up unknowns at your altitude. Any visuals?"

*

"Negative, control," Captain Wesselman said. "Southeast skies are clear."

"Good. Bring up the bird and continue to twenty thousand. How's the fuel?" Ritchie asked.

"Fuel's not a concern for a few hours," Wesselman said.

"Circle and await further instructions," Ritchie said.

"Roger, over and out." Wesselman adjusted the mic on his headset when a sudden movement in his left peripheral stopped him. *What was that?* Whatever it was, it was gone now.

He turned to Hall. "You inform the passengers. I don't need the distraction."

Without hesitation, Hall picked up the mic and pressed the button labeled *cabin* on the control panel. "Ladies and gentlemen: this is your First Officer, Jim Hall. The folks at MSY had a change of plans for us. So if you're wondering why we stopped descending and have leveled out, you'll be pleased to know it has nothing to do with the plane's mechanics. I'm sure MSY will resolve the problem they are experiencing as soon as they can. In the meantime, the Captain will bring us up to twenty thousand feet, and we'll circle until permitted to land. The *fasten seatbelt* sign will stay on until we touchdown. Thank you for your patience and understanding. And remember when it comes to flying, *Delta is ready when you are*."

Hall looked over at Wesselman. "How was that?"

Wesselman smirked. "Textbook, son."

Hall's chest swole as a prideful smile curved over his lips. "Thank you, sir."

"Don't get too cocky. *Textbook* can get you killed. You have to trust your intuition as much as your training. There will be times in your piloting career where you'll have to veer from protocol to save your jet."

"IIow will I know when it's time to abandon protocol?" Hall asked.

"Well, you won't know *when* to avoid protocol. You'll only know after you violate it if you've made the right call or not." Wesselman let the comment hang in the air without any further elaboration. A pilot had to learn when to trust his intuition, and, there were no guarantees in life.

Hall stared blankly at the cockpit window. His face slowly lost color.

*

"I don't care if Delta is ready to *fly* when I am. I want Delta to *land* when it's supposed to," a portly man, who had seen the brighter sides of youth years ago, announced to no one in particular. From the beginning of the flight, he had mouthed an unlit cigar, rolling the turd-like object from side to side in his mouth.

Kathy Stevens sat securely in her jump seat, doing her best to ignore the obnoxious passenger's random comments. From the time he had stepped on the plane, he acted as if he were the only person in the cabin. About every five minutes, he had made a rhetorical statement loud enough for half of those riding in coach to hear.

As if that quirk wasn't bad enough, he took the liberty to un-jail the confinement of his sweaty toes and had removed his shoes. The funky smell hovered in the air like a thick fog. Thus, earning him a special name in her mind, *Stinky*. She so wished she could have let him *have it* for being so rude. Instead, she forced a fake smile and thought about that extra week of vacation she'd be getting in a few months when she reached her tenth anniversary as a flight attendant for Delta.

At least she wasn't held hostage like the bearded young man sitting to Stinky's right, by the window. The young man leaned at a forty-five-degree angle away from him for the duration of the trip. Stinky had lifted the armrest between them. His fat thighs and bloated gut encroached the young man's personal space to the point of physical contact.

Snap-snap. Stinky had clicked his fingers together and said, "Hey, you."

She resisted the urge to look Stinky's *way* in the hope he was speaking to someone else.

Snapping his fingers again, Stinky called out, "Stewardess."

Kathy darted her gaze sideways through narrow eyelids. *No one* called flight attendants stewardesses anymore. Would he have called a male flight attendant *stewardess*? Strike three for Stinky in Kathy's book. "Can I help you, sir?" She realized her tone was a little less than pleasant and hoped Stinky was smart enough to get the veiled message.

"Yeah," Stinky said and removed the cigar from his mouth with his left hand and held the wet end toward the ceiling. "Am I going to make my connection?"

You might as well have asked me for the winning lottery numbers. Maintaining her professionalism, she said, "I don't have that information, sir. What time does your departing flight leave?"

"It leaves forty-five minutes from now."

"Sir, even if we didn't have a landing delay, there would be no way for me to assure you would make your connecting flight. You should always plan at least for a two-hour layover between flights."

"I paid big bucks for a ticket that had the times of arrival and departure plainly printed on them. If the airlines kept their schedule, there wouldn't be any problems making my connection."

"Sir, I assure you all the airlines do their best to keep the planes running on time. Delays cost the airlines money as well as displeasing their customers," Kathy said, thinking the man had the reasoning ability of an eight-year-old.

"How's about a shot of whiskey then when we level out? Put it on the Captain's tab for—"

BAM!

The Boeing 737 jolted, slinging the passengers forward, and Kathy backward—ramming the back of her head into the partition. People screamed, children and babies cried, and the jet's right wing dipped.

*

"Flameout right engine!" Jim Hall yelled from the co-pilot's seat.

"Son-of-a-gun! We've hit something! Get that engine restarted, pilot!" Wesselman commanded, keeping a tight grip on the control wheel with his left hand while his right adjusted the throttle. "Come on, baby. Hang in there. You can do this," he said in a low voice.

The situation was dire, but it was no time to panic. This is where all those countless hours of training paid off. A pilot never stops piloting the plane—no matter what! At least they had only lost one engine. Limping into an emergency landing was a walk in the park compared to losing both engines.

Wesselman watched his altitude indicator as he smoothly lifted the right wing out of the roll and trimmed the rudder, leveling the jet again.

"The engine's not responding, sir. We're losing fuel," Hall said, he heaved air in and out like he had run a marathon.

"Shutting fuel off right engine now," Wesselman said as he flipped a switch on the panel. "Get back on the radio and explain the situation to MSY. Tell them we already have a route plotted for Lakefront and to get us in over there pronto!"

*

"AHH! It's the monster from Twilight Zone on the wing!" Stinky yelled as he unsuccessfully tried to stand, his seatbelt holding him firmly in place.

"Sir! Calm down. You're scaring the other passengers," Kathy yelled as another round of screams followed Stinky's outburst. She had no idea what he was talking about, as the passenger obscured her view of the right wing.

"That's not a monster. That's a pterosaur," the young man next to Stinky said. "See the head and the wing? The head's triangular shaped at the top, and its bill is long and flat. There're about ninety conical shaped teeth that are larger near the jaw and get smaller at the front of its beak. Most people erroneously refer to any pterosaur as a *Pterodactyl*. *Pterodactyl*, from the Greek, means *winged-finger*."

"We're all about to die here, and you wanna give me a lecture on dinosaurs? Hey Einstein, how's about you put a lid on it?" Stinky said, somehow managing to keep the cigar in his mouth.

"How did you know my name?" the young man asked.

"What? Your name really is *Einstein*?" Stinky said.

"Dave Einstein. I'm a student at Tulane University," Dave said. "Oh, and pterosaurs aren't dinosaurs. They're reptiles. They were the only flying reptiles known to exist."

The plane had leveled, and the passengers silently caught their breath when the Captain's voice came over the radio:

"Ladies and Gentleman: this is Captain Wesselman. I apologize for the rough ride. We've unfortunately struck some birds or another foreign object with our right engine. The engine is no longer operational, but that is no cause for alarm. We can fly safely with one engine with little to no additional risk on landing. MSY has cleared us to set down on the Lakefront airport in fifteen minutes. Please remain seated and calm until touchdown. Again, I apologize for the inconvenience."

The passengers in the cabin had quieted for the most part, with only a wail of an infant pricking nerves already set on edge.

Kathy removed the cabin mic from its perch, but before she followed protocol, Stinky said:

"Can I go to the bathroom?"

Rolling her eyes and wanting to curse him in three different languages, she said, "No, I'm sorry, sir. It's not safe for you to leave your seat."

"But I really need to go."

"No, you can't do that."

"Well then, can you get me one of those little bottles of whiskey? I don't need ice or anything. I'll drink it straight."

With possible death only a few minutes away, Kathy ignored the buffoon, keyed the mic, and said, "Ladies and Gentlemen: Even though the captain doesn't expect any problems upon landing, we must take every precaution for our safety. At this time, please check again for any loose objects and secure them underneath your seats.

"A life jacket is in the pocket under your seat cushion. Pull the jacket out and place it over your head. Clip on the waistband and pull it tight. Please do not inflate it while you are still inside the aircraft. An evacuation slide and life raft are at each door. The crew will direct you to your door.

"Before we land, I will tell you to assume the *brace* position. You will lower your heads to your knees and keep your legs tucked straight and un-crossed. We're trying to avoid broken bones, so you must be sure to assume the brace position. I'll tell everyone to do this when the time is right."

BAM!

Something hit the jet again, throwing the passengers forward and Kathy backward. The cabin mic fell from her hand.

"My God!" a woman's voice called out. "The left engine's missing!"

*

"Flameout left engine!" Hall said as the *engine starting manual* dropped from his hand. "We're going down!"

That what Wesselman had feared the most had come upon him. He was three thousand feet in the sky with no engines to fly them to safety. The two hundred-thousand-pound jet needed thrust to stay afloat in the sea of air. Now, the 737 was essentially a glider without the means to catch air currents that could send them higher. The jet had become a flying anchor with wings.

"Captain? What are we going to do? We're too low and too far from MSY or Lakefront to land!" Hall cried out.

Wesselman's mind raced with options for a makeshift runway. The interstate system was a crowded mess as always. There were no vacant fields large enough in Louisiana's most populated city to put the bird down. There was only one option that he saw. He shifted the wing flaps and trimmed the rudder, pointing the nose of the jet toward the Mississippi River.

"MSY, this is Delta two-thirty-six. We've lost thrust on both engines. No time for us to reach you or Lakefront. I'm putting us down in the Mississippi," Wesselman said over the radio.

"The Mississippi! You can't do that," the control tower said.

"It's all I've got," Wesselman said. Spare seconds were few. No time to argue with a controller who didn't have an imminent fear of dying in a fiery explosion. He needed his full wits if he had any hopes of saving the lives of his passengers. "Inform the Coast Guard. We have one hundred and twenty-two passengers and crew. I expect to save them all."

"Copy, two-thirty-six. Godspeed."

"The Mississippi River? Who do you think you are, *Sully Sullenberger*?" Hall said, the previous admiration of his captain void in his tone.

"What do you want me to do? Land on Canal Street and park next to Harrah's Casino for a round of blackjack?"

"But we'll all die!"

"Get ahold of yourself, man!" Wesselman commanded. "I'll have you know I was one of the pilots who flew the simulator for evidence at Sullenberger's trial."

With eyes widened and hope in his voice, Hall said, "You did? So you learned what you needed to do to land on water?"

"No, I crashed. But, I learned what not to do. You're just going to have to trust me."

Ding. Ding. Ding. (The Flight Warning System began its incessant chime.)

Too low. Terrain, the Ground Proximity System announced.

The nose of the 737 now pointed in line with the winding river.

"The bridge! You're heading toward the Mississippi River bridge!" Hall said, panicked.

"The river is too curvy to go the other way. I need as straight of a shot as I can get."

Too low. Gear.

"We're not going to clear the bridge!" Hall said.

"Shut up and tell me our speed."

"One hundred and fifty knots, sir," Hall said, seemingly distracted by the menial task.

Good, Wesselman knew the speed. He wanted Hall to focus on something else.

Terrain terrain. Pull up. Pull up.

"We're going to hit! We're going to hit!" Hall screamed.

"Brace for impact," Wesselman announced over the radio.

The jet no longer seemed to fly. Instead, it drifted slowly between the two towers of the Mississippi River Bridge, over the horizontal trusses in the middle. If the wheels were lowered, Wesselman doubted they would have cleared the trusses.

With the muddy waters of the Mississippi looming before them like a dark highway to death, Wesselman prepared to set the metallic bird down.

*

"Brace for impact!" the Captain's voice said over the cabin's speakers.

Kathy was still disoriented from the second hit on the back of the head. Her duty now was to warn the passengers in a constant chant to brace for impact; like a drummer pacing strokes on a dragon boat.

"Brace for impact. Brace for impact. Brace for impact. Brace for impact."

She recognized Sharon Henderson's voice over the cabin speaker. Sharon and Jayla Watkins were the other two flight attendants on-board. Kathy didn't like Sharon taking over her duties, but she guessed her delay at giving the warning prompted Sharon to move to action.

"Brace! Brace! Brace! Brace!" Sharon called out again.

With her feet flat on the floor, and her arms tight against her thighs with her head in her lap, the plane hit the water.

There was a tremendous splash, and the impact jarred her head again.

Passengers let out a chorus of death screams.

Kathy knew the end was imminent. Her mind's eye saw the jet break apart and rolling flames in an all-consuming inferno engulf everyone and everything.

*

The jet hadn't stopped its forward progression on water when Wesselman unlatched his seat belt and jumped out his chair. Now was not the time to reflect how lucky they were to get this far. The plane could quickly take water and drown everyone on board! How ironic would that be?

"Radio in that we've made it. Then, get up and get the passengers out!" Wesselman said to Hall as he opened the door to first class seating.

Hall was still in the crash position but snapped to attention and grabbed the seat buckle at the captain's command.

Ignoring the questions and calls from the passengers in first class, Wesselman went straight to the front right passenger door and opened it. The waves of the muddy Mississippi threatened to steal their lives but were still several feet below.

"Not on my watch," Wesselman said through gritted teeth. He deployed an inflatable slide and watched it unfold and grow into a temporary refuge. "Everyone, calmly leave your seats and file out in an orderly fashion. We have plenty of time before the plane takes on too much water. The Coast Guard is on its way to pick us up. Remember to inflate your life vest when you get on the slide."

Jim Hall exited the cockpit and stepped over to the left passenger door, throwing it open, and deploying the inflatable slide.

Wesselman snaked down the aisle before it became impassable with bodies and burst through the curtain separating first class from coach. He was pleased to see all four mid-cabin emergency doors were open and people had begun to step out onto the wings.

Kathy Stevens helped an elderly lady from her seat, and the other two flight attendants herded the others out from the rear of the plane.

"Any injuries?" he asked Kathy, though her back was to him.

"I don't think anything more than bumps and bruises. The people just want to get out and worry what's broken later."

Fear did have a way of masking pain. Wesselman had heard many soldiers' stories of getting hit during a firefight and not realizing it until after it was over. He was amazed how calm the people were. He'd seen more frenzied passengers on a *normal* arrival; trying to be the first ones out.

"You did a great job landing, Captain!" a man cried out from the rear.

Mild applause and a few verbal affirmations let him know others felt that way too.

"I'm still gonna miss my connecting flight," an overweight man with an unlit cigar in his mouth complained, not bothering to look the captain in the eye.

Wesselman poked his head back in first class to find it empty and Hall looking out the right side of the passenger door.

"The Coast Guard is almost here. There are tugboats coming to the rescue too," Hall said.

For the first time, tension released in Wesselman's back. He took in a breath of river air and thought he could smell Cajun spices mixed with roasting pork. What he wouldn't give for a hurricane from Pat O'Leary's right now!

"Go out and help the passengers get on the boats. Leave with the last of them," Wesselman said.

"Yes, sir," Hall said without a protest.

Jim Hall was a good man and would one day be a good pilot, Wesselman thought. Hall still had much to learn before he earned a Captain's hat. His flight experience didn't include a military foundation to make him a warrior. That was a big disadvantage. Being a warrior taught Wesselman how to be a survivor. A survivor knows what it takes to win, no matter the cost.

The minutes ticked by and shortly the plane was void of its passengers. Water was less than a foot away from spilling into the cabin, and most of the passengers were already safely aboard other vessels.

He was the Captain, and there was no way he could leave without being one hundred percent sure there was no one left behind.

Starting from the cockpit, he went down the aisle checking bathrooms and between seats, the galley, and the small areas designated for the crew only.

After the first pass, he repeated the process. That's what it took for him to allow himself to leave his plane to her watery grave. "You did good," he said as he patted the fuselage by the door opening.

Stepping out and onto the wing, water wet the bottom of his shoes.

Three Coast Guard vessels and four tugboats set fifty or so yards away. The last of the passengers taking a boat that ferried them from the plane were just about to get off.

Thomas Wesselman looked up to the sky and gave thanks. He had peace and a calm unlike anything else he had ever felt. The weight of the universe lifted from his shoulders.

Cheers and waves erupted from the people on the boats. Many jumped with joy, and a few waved US flags.

Wesselman smiled the width of the Mississippi and waved back. Despite the near horrific tragedy, this was the happiest day in his life.

The dark water bubbled just to his left in front of the wing. In a split second, a mouth as large as a car sprang from the water. It looked similar to an alligator's but was more round than long. Water slung as its jaws opened, hitting Wesselman in the face, and revealing teeth as large as railroad spikes.

With no time to move, the mouth closed, ushering instant darkness. Wesselman's conscious quickly eroded, but not before teeth mangled soft flesh and jaws crushed bone in an explosion of agonizing pain.

*

Half of the crowd screamed, and the other half stood with mouths agape. The captain was there one second, and then he was gone, snatched from the wing by a large creature from the depths of the Mississippi River.

"I knew they had big catfish in the Mississippi River, but that was ridiculous," Stinky said over the stunned silence.

"Hmm," Dave Einstein said. "That wasn't a catfish. It was a mosasaur from the Cretaceous period. Interesting…"

With an incredulous look on his face, Stinky said, "Yeah, well I know what *mosasaur* means from the Greek." Before Dave had a chance to reply, Stinky said, "It means *shut your yap*, you self-absorbed, millennium snowflake!"

In the distance, the steam whistle of the paddlewheeler Southern Queen announced it was about to begin its four-hour adventure down the mighty Mississippi.

CHAPTER 3

Bridget Reed had her hand under Dr. Bryan Breaux's head as the clouds dissipated in his mind from the effects of the quantum transportation device. Breaux's eyes sparkled with life.

"Bridget, I've been on the most amazing journey," the professor said.

Having one's brain disassembled and 3D printed back in place probably introduced a lot of confusion. "I've been right here with you the whole time, Doc. You're looking good. How do you feel?"

"No, I've been gone for weeks...perhaps months." Breaux's tongue slid between his lips. "Back in time...millions...hundreds of millions of years." He turned his head and looked Bridget in the eyes. "Something went wrong with the quantum transport. Q created a time-wave and sent me back to prehistoric times. I...I lived among long-extinct creatures...mostly hiding. But I never stayed in one place very long. The time-wave kept shifting and shifting. Until..." he reached out with his right hand and touched Bridget on the arm, "until now."

"We need to get you to a hospital. Do you want me to call nine-one-one?"

With renewed strength in his voice, he said, "No." He then lifted from the floor with his left elbow and sat upright, quickly covering his private parts with the hand he had removed from Bridget's arm.

"In fact," Breaux continued, "I don't think I need to go to the hospital at all. At least, I mean today."

"I don't know, Dr. Breaux. Your body has just gone through a traumatic experience. Checking into a hospital where they can measure your vitals is in your best interest."

"What do you want me to say? *Hello, I've just been demolecularized and reassembled. Can you please take my temperature and blood pressure?*"

"Tell them you have complications from pancreatic cancer. You are dying, you know," Bridget said, regretting her words might have come out too insensitive.

A boyish smirk curled on Breaux's lips. "Cancer? What cancer? I don't have cancer anymore."

"But you can't know that," Bridget said and stood. "I'm beginning to think the transportation *has* affected your brain."

"I wrote the program that replaced all the cancer cells with normal cells. I know it worked. Plus," Breaux brought his left hand up to his chest, "Plus, the *demon* is gone."

"The *demon*? What are you talking about now? Some New Orleans Voodoo baloney?"

"Not hardly. One morning I woke up, before I knew I had cancer, and I knew something was not right in my body. I ignored it at first. After a few weeks, I broke down and went to the doctor, of which my tests showed negative. Still, I felt like something wicked resided inside. The cancer finally progressed enough to show up in tests. From that point on, I've called that feeling *my demon*."

"And that feeling is gone?"

"Yes, Bridget. That feeling...my *demon* is gone!" Breaux said victoriously. "Now, if you would excuse me, I'd like to get dressed."

"I'll give you all the space you need, Doc. I'm going to wash my face and get a Coke from the break room. I need some relief." Bridget turned and left.

"I need some relief too. Bridget, I'm taking you to the Quarter, and we are going to celebrate."

"Don't you think you're pushing things?" She called back while still walking away. "Why don't you go home and celebrate?"

"Because I don't want to be alone, and I want you to come. You helped save me!"

"Do you need me around because you're worried you might have complications from the experiment?"

"No, I want you to come because I might get too drunk. You might have to drive me home."

*

Dr. Bryan Breaux shut down his aging Volvo in the Parking Lot next to the historic Jax Brewery in the French Quarter. The brewery and bottle house's run lasted from 1891 to the mid-1970s, actually becoming the largest brewery in the south at one point. Financial problems had forced Jax to sell to a competitor. Now, the converted brewery had a variety of specialty shops, retail stores, and restaurants serving food with a Creole flair.

"This is the most expensive parking lot in the Quarter," Bridget said after she and the professor exited the vehicle and headed for Jackson Square. "I usually park down by the French Market. Plenty of free parking over there."

"Eh, that's too far away. I have a new lease on life, and I don't want to waste the precious time I've left on Earth to save a few dollars."

Passing through the lot entrance and waiting for an opportunity to cross Decatur Street, a distinctive Lucky Dog cart caught his peripheral. The cart was shaped like a hot dog on the bun and slathered in rich mustard. The proprietor hadn't seen the edge of a razor in quite some time. His dingy white jacket had a combination of ketchup red, mustard yellow, and relish green splatters that would have earned a spot in a Jackson Pollock exhibition. The *lady* in the blue dress he spoke to had a beard and fairy wings.

"I've lived in New Orleans for over ten years, been to the Quarter countless times, and I've never once had a Lucky Dog," Dr. Breaux said.

"I've had them before. You're not missing out on anything."

"But if I don't eat one, then I'll never have that experience. I don't want to die without knowing what a Lucky Dog tastes like."

"The experience might just kill you. Don't you see how filthy that vendor looks? Lucky Dog's are drunk food anyway. You aren't drunk yet."

"Well then, we might have to make a stop here on the way back."

"Whatever," Bridget said, sounding in no mood for a petty argument.

"Hey, buddy?" the vendor said. "I saw you lookin' over here. You want me to fix you up with a Lucky Dog?"

The professor shifted his gaze back to the vendor, and said, "I'm sorry, sir. I think I will take a pass on that. Maybe later."

The vendor shrugged, and the bearded lady next to him asked, "How about *my* lucky dog?" She lifted her blue skirt high enough to reveal that she wasn't wearing any underwear.

Feeling a rush of blood to his face, Breaux said, "Uh, ah, no thanks. No thank you. I'm going to pass on that too." Seeing an opening in the traffic, he grabbed Bridget's hand and led her across the street.

"What? You aren't going to try out *that* lucky dog?" Bridget asked and then giggled.

"Not what I had in mind," Breaux said.

"But what about the experience? You may *die* never knowing what *that* lucky dog was like."

"You've made your point. Not all experiences are prudent."

They took the sidewalk a short block away to Jackson Square, passing several donkey driven carriages with accommodating carriage drivers bubbling with enthusiasm, ready to take a rider on a historical tour of the city.

Dr. Breaux slowed his pace, and said, "You know, all the years I've been here, I haven't taken a carriage ride."

"Are you going to start up again? I thought you wanted to get a drink? We're not on a date. If you want me to stick around, you better anchor me down with a cocktail," Bridget said, as she took the lead and pulled him along.

They reached the corner of St. Peter Street, which ran on the west side of the block wide, wrought-iron fenced Jackson Square. Pat O'Leary's was just over a block away.

Turning, restaurants and other specialty stores lined the left side of the street. On the right side, various artists had set up shop, hanging their wares on the iron fencing, ready for purchase at a special price. A Tarot card reader or two had tables open with an empty chair waiting to show the next customer their inevitable future.

The noise level coming from inside the Square was much higher than normal.

"Did you know the architects designed Jackson Square after the seventeenth-century *Place des Vosges* in Paris?" Breaux asked.

"No, I didn't," Bridget said. "I just assumed they built the Square around the statue of Andrew Jackson after the Battle of New Orleans in eighteen-fourteen."

"The statue itself didn't go up until eighteen-fifty-one," Breaux said. "The Battle of New Orleans officially started on December fourteenth, eighteen-fourteen. Ironically, ten days later on the twenty-fourth, Great Britain and the United States signed a treaty that effectively ended the War of eighteen-twelve. News was slow to travel then, and Congress didn't ratify the agreement until February sixteenth, eighteen-fifteen."

"Are you a big history buff?" Bridget asked.

"Me? No, not particularly. I read up on the history of New Orleans when I moved here. I, uh, have sort of a photographic memory. Sorry, I didn't mean to bore you."

"You're not boring me. At least you aren't trying to buy every piece of art here so you *won't miss the experience*."

"Okay, Bridget. I've learned my lesson."

"Read your fortune, sir?" A young woman with porcelain white makeup on her face asked. Her ashen hair flowed down from underneath a purple scarf wrapped around her head. Black lipstick perfectly covered her plump lips.

"No, thank you," Bridget said.

"Wait." Breaux slowed his pace and veered over to her table.

"Have a seat, and Madam Tiffany will read your past and tell you the future," the fortune teller said.

"Dr. Breaux?" Bridget protested.

"Just one minute," he said to his student. "Madam Tiffany, if I told you I had just traveled back in time millions of years ago, where I dodged dinosaurs and other extinct creatures for weeks, would your cards see that?"

"Of course not. The cards only deal with reality," Madam Tiffany said.

"Then I suggest you find another line of work. Because," Dr. Breaux had leaned in and locked gazes with the fortune teller, "*it's true*." Right now, he wasn't in the mood for someone to manipulate his emotions—try to play on weakness and give false hope. Life was too short for such silliness.

"Dr. Breaux, Pat O's is calling. I'm going with or without you." Bridget let go of his hand and soldiered on.

Breaux lifted a pointed finger to Madam Tiffany, and said, "It's true." He turned and hurried off after Bridget, not waiting for a response.

He caught up with her right at the west gates leading to the Square. A much larger crowd than regular tourists lined up around Andrew Jackson's statue. Chanting from one group began, and then another group responded with their rebuttal. The two sides fervently strained to drown out the other.

"What's going on in there?" Breaux asked.

"I think that's the group called *Tear Them to the Ground*. They're protesting Andrew Jackson's statue."

"Andrew Jackson? I understood the reasoning behind removing the Confederate statues, though I didn't take a stance on the issues. The City removed those statues a few months ago. Why would anyone want General Jackson's statue taken down?"

"Jackson owned slaves, and the statue is a sign of white supremacy, or so says Rev. Martin Scott, the leader of Tear Them to the Ground. The group is protesting tax dollars spent on maintaining any remnant of white supremacy."

"Woah, taking a stance of that magnitude is going to open a huge can of worms. Seems a bit extreme, but I don't have the history of being an African American to fully understand that perspective.

"Bridget, do you feel that way? Do you want to see historical figures torn down because of a past way of life? The statue doesn't honor Jackson for owning slaves. He was the leader in the Battle of New Orleans and the seventh president of the United States, for God's sake."

"Me, Doc? I don't allow any wrongdoing of the past affect my way of life today. I don't have that kind of time to waste worrying about what I had no control over. I worry about *today*—what I can do to move my people and me forward. That said, it doesn't bother me the Confederate statues are gone. But, someone needs to draw a line how far things should go. I think removing the statue of Jackson is extreme."

Bryan Breaux liked to think of himself as being open-minded. But if he looked deep inside, he rarely made more than a cursory effort to put himself in *the other person's shoes*—to see and feel reality from an opposing viewpoint. "I think in the past I've been too quick to judge others. My new lease on life has made me aware that I've got a lot of soul-searching to do."

"I do some of my best soul-searching over a cocktail," Bridget said. "We're here."

A tall man wearing coattails in front of Pat O'leary's spotted them. He tipped his hat and motioned with his arm for them to *come right on in.*

*

Dr. Breaux sat on the patio of Pat O'Leary's at a small table near a brick wall with a couple of ornamental trees growing in front of it. Tiki torches placed strategically on the walls added ambiance.

The humidity hung thick in the Louisiana afternoon, but a nearby fan kept enough artificial breeze blowing on the back of his neck for it not to spoil his afternoon.

In the center of the patio, which had nearly every table made of glass and iron filled with tourists and locals, a *flaming fountain* majestically set the mood. Streams of water falling from the copper and stone fountain acted as gentle background music mixed with the hum of others having a good time. The brilliant flame shooting amongst the cascading streams would add a warm glow to the sky as darkness fell.

"Too bad we couldn't get a seat in the piano bar," Breaux said. "You can hear those people laughing and singing from out here."

"That place is too crowded. The main bar too. I'm enjoying the patio," Bridget said. "You aren't having a good time?"

"Oh, I'm having a great time. As evidence, I'm on my third hurricane," Breaux said. "I guess all this rum makes me want to let loose a bit."

"Don't get too loose. You might fall apart," Bridget said and giggled. "There's four ounces of rum in each one of those drinks."

"Do you know why these drinks are called *hurricanes*?"

"No, I guess because we live in the south and these drinks are potent enough to blow you away like a hurricane."

"Why they are potent, the name came from the glass Pat O'leary's serves the drink in. Notice," he ran his finger from the top of his drink to the bottom. "The glass replicates an old hurricane lamp."

"That's interesting, but that takes away some of the mystique of the drink for me."

"Not to me. Knowing that bit of added history enhances my appreciation for the hurricane. Plus, I'm a scientist. I like to be informed," Breaux said.

"I'm a scientist, and I like drinks that blow me away."

The two laughed.

"I think these hurricanes are getting the job done," Breaux said before picking up his drink and poking the straw between his searching lips.

Something whizzed by his head, catching his right peripheral, and landed on a branch of one of the nearby ornamental trees.

At first, Breaux thought a bat had flown by, because of the way the creature flapped its wings. It was small—about the size of a sparrow. From that distance, and what the professor could make out, it wasn't either a bird or a bat.

The creature didn't have feathers or hair. Its tan wings looked leathery like a bat's, but its distinct teardrop shaped head and long beak appeared to be more bird-like. The body, though, had both front arms and rear legs, though the front arms were a bit shorter. Wings folded upward at the front arms, jutting up over the creature's back.

"Bridget?"

"What, Doc?"

"Over there, the tree on the left. Do you see what's sitting on that branch?" Breaux asked.

"Sorry, Doc. My contacts were bothering me, and I took them out when we got here. I can see up close, but my distance is blurry. What is it?"

"I'm not sure," Breaux said. "It almost looks like a bat with a bird's head, but—"

The creature dove from the branch and landed on the table, right between Bridget and Breaux.

Both sat silent. Their gazes fixated on the uninvited guest.

"Doc, that's not a bird," Bridget said.

"I know. It's a reptile."

"A reptile with wings?"

"Yes, a reptile with wings. It's a pterosaur."

"A pterosaur?"

"Yes, and pterosaurs have been extinct for millions of years," Breaux said, a familiar feeling crept up his spine. Unnerving fear just like he had felt when the quantum transporter had sent him back in prehistoric times.

The joyful notes wafting from ivory keys striking metal strings of the piano ended in a thunder of screams coming from the inside bars.

The tiny pterosaur left its table perch and flew to a fence rail, where it greedily devoured an unsuspecting brown gecko.

All heads jutted toward the carriageway where the slate flooring had led them to the patio.

A creature as big as a medium-sized dog scurried from the carriageway onto the patio and slid to a halt. It looked like another reptile/bird combination; with the head light blue and looking lizard-like on a short neck. A brown feathered crest on its crown matched the feathers on its body. It had small wings on short arms that would make it impossible for it to take flight. Most noticeable were the claws on its hands and feet. The nails looked deadly enough to shred alligator hide.

"That's not a rooster," Bridget said as the patio patrons pointed and gasped.

"It's a *velociraptor*, and pound for pound, it's one of the deadliest creatures to ever exist."

The velociraptor stood high on its back legs and darted its gaze about until it chose its target and sprang for a kill.

An aging man, identified as a tourist by his souvenir t-shirt and a collection of Mardis Gras beads around his neck, howled like a stuck pig when the velociraptor landed on his head.

The dinosaur's leg claws sank into the man's chest just below his chin. The front claws slashed in wild abandon, tearing flesh, slinging blood, and gouging his eyes out.

Pandemonium erupted, with screams and cries from terror-stricken patrons who had one of two means of exit from the patio blocked.

The man's wife was on her feet crying out as much as her husband. She, though, wasn't going to let the velociraptor win without a fight. It wasn't much of a weapon, but she repeatedly smashed the dinosaur with her purse, all the while cursing it with words that would make a sailor blush.

Breaux and Bridget were both on their feet—trying to determine their next move!

The professor estimated there were at least three hundred patrons searching to escape the patio. The carriageway had filled, as some party-goers streamed in from the front bars, cutting off the view of the poor man fighting for his life. The mass hysteria ensured a great possibility for self-induced injuries.

"This is crazy, Doc. We need to get out of here!" Bridget yelled.

The brick patio walls were at least fifteen feet tall at the lowest point. There wasn't a way to make a quick exit. Although, a bar area close to one wall had a sloping tin roof that Breaux thought they might reach by climbing from a table top.

A horrific snarl cut through the panicked cries, and a dinosaur about half the size of a grown man fast-stepped onto the patio from the carriageway. It was a theropod, probably a *troodon*. It had long, slender legs with raised sickle-shaped claws on the inside of feet. The head and body were reptilian, stretching at least six feet in length, and over three feet in height. Its olive-green skin had golden stripes marking its spine.

"I've got a bad feeling about this, Bridget," Breaux said as people scattered away from the approaching troodon. "We need to get to the other side by the bar."

"But there's no exit there, and that dinosaur is between us and the bar!"

"Look at the roof. It's lower. We can reach it by climbing from a table." Realizing time was short, he sprinted and grabbed a tiki torch on the wall. The anemic flame would do little to scare the dinosaur. How Breaux wished he could use the flame from the fountain for their defense. Turning the screw and lengthening the wick, the flame burned four times bigger. It would have to do. "Get behind me," he said as he rejoined Bridget by their table.

Dr. Breaux kept the torch near his chest as people fled past him, careful not to accidentally burn anyone or himself. He and Bridget were the only people heading in the troodon's direction, and that didn't go unnoticed.

The dinosaur's eyes widened, and it hissed out a cry of warning or delight, eager to meet the oncoming humans.

With the path clear between them, Breaux held the torch at arms' length to keep the predator at a distance.

"That flame's not big enough to kill it," Bridget said.

"I'm not trying to kill it. I'm just trying to keep it away so we can make our escape."

As Breaux poked the flame in the troodon's face, close enough to singe its nostrils, the dinosaur pulled back in obvious fear. It also let out an unusual cry that was either out of pain or being pissed off.

Didn't matter. Breaux quickly side-stepped with the torch keeping a less than comfortable distance between them and the dinosaur.

The troodon's ire increased, and it repeatedly snapped at the torch each time it poked its way.

"We're almost there," Breaux said. "Push the closest table underneath the edge of the roof."

Standing his ground, Breaux kept the torch waving to-and-fro in front of him. The screech of iron on slate told him Bridget would soon have a means for their escape in place.

The troodon bobbed and weaved like a feisty boxer.

Breaux wondered how long before the dinosaur would move past its fear of the fire and attack.

"It's ready, Doc!" Bridget called out.

"Get on the table and onto the roof!"

"But what about you?"

"Don't worry about me. I'll find a way."

The troodon pulled its head back and waited for the torch to sling by, and then jutted its head and bit the torch on the handle below the flaming head.

Not good! Breaux tried to jerk it from the dinosaur's mouth, but he didn't have the strength. The troodon tried to pull the torch from his grasp, but he held on for everything he was worth. This was a bad situation that he didn't see getting out of. At least Bridget would get away.

A vodka bottle smashed in front of the dinosaur, wetting it and the floor underneath it. Almost instantly, the torch ignited the liquid and engulfed the troodon in a yellow-orange flame.

"Now we can leave together," Bridget said. She stepped onto a chair and onto the table.

Breaux let the torch fall from his hand and scampered over to the table. Bridget had just pulled herself up on the roof when he reached the chair.

A few seconds later, the two sat from above and watched as more dinosaurs rushed onto the patio. A sea of people fought to get out. He didn't know if the other exit was blocked or if in the turmoil human bodies had plugged the only means of escape.

They stood on the roof and cried out for others to follow, but the ensuing carnage of dinosaurs tearing people to shreds prevented anyone else from following their path.

"It's...horrible," Bridget said. "I can't believe this is happening. This can't be happening."

Breaux watched with his jaw hanging down to his chest. He didn't know how to rationally accept the situation. There was no denying, though, as blood splattered and death cries reverberated off the brick walls, that this was all too real.

Bridget stood by his side. "Dr. Breaux...what have we done?"

CHAPTER 4

Kathy Stevens and Jayla Watkins dutifully met, consoled, and directed the airline passengers as each stepped off the rescuing vessels. The Coast Guard boats and tugboats had docked at the Canal Street Ferry Terminal and unloaded their human cargo.

Most of the passengers went through the motions like glassy-eyed zombies and headed like cattle to a staging area close to the paddlewheeler Southern Queen's dock.

Kathy was in shock but managed to function on auto-pilot. In her mind, she kept seeing Captain Wesselman standing on the plane's wing, waving. The monstrosity appeared from the river in an instant—its alligator-like mouth engulfing the captain, and just like that, Wesselman was gone.

Dave Einstein had called the creature a dinosaur. A *mosasaur*, if she recalled correctly. Dinosaurs didn't exist in modern times; especially in the Mississippi River. Seeing was believing, though. And that flying creature that smashed into the engine was from prehistoric times, too.

Sharon Henderson had abandoned her duties as a flight attendant and spent her time consoling co-pilot, Jim Hall. Sharon was near twice the first officer's age and had a notorious reputation for going after young meat. Her display of *comfort* was well over the top.

Leave the poor boy alone, old woman, Kathy thought. If Sharon weren't so efficient at her job, Kathy would have no reason to like her at all.

The passengers had gathered in a semi-circle around Hall, who had to adjust the crooked reading glasses on his ears disheveled by Sharon's hugs. Looking at his electronic tablet, he said, "Uh, ladies, and gentleman. We've just been through the biggest scare of our lives. I am pleased to say we've made it safe and sound to the earth, thanks to the valiant efforts and expert flying of Captain Thomas Wesselman. God rest his soul.

"As to what or where the creature who took the captain's life came from, I have no explanation. If I hadn't seen the sudden attack with my own two eyes, I wouldn't have believed it possible. Hopefully, the Coast Guard will find whatever did this and destroy it."

Blank expressions looked at the first officer. Several people sniffed and cleared their throats. One woman sobbed softly into her hands.

Hall brought his gaze up for a few moments and then focused back on his tablet. "I have some more bad news. For reasons not reported, the Louis Armstrong New Orleans International Airport has suspended all incoming and outgoing flights at this time."

An excited and discontented murmur grew amongst the crowd.

"I'm authorized to bring everyone over to The River Walk," Hall said and lifted a pointed finger to his right. The huge riverfront mall was fifty yards away. "The airline is sending representatives to the mall where they will give you vouchers for lodging, transportation, and will then reschedule your flights."

"Why is the airport closed down? Is it terrorists?" Stinky asked with both fists implanted to the side of his hips.

"Sir, I'm sorry, but as I said, the reason is undisclosed." Hall stared at Stinky for several moments without anyone else asking a question they knew he wouldn't have an answer to. "Now, because the New Orleans airport is on lock-down, our representatives are coming from Baton Rouge. That means it will take several hours before a team can assemble and make the drive down here. In the meantime, there are restroom facilities and restaurants in the River Walk. Delta will pick up the tab for any food and refreshments you might need."

"Are you buying us cocktails too?" Stinky asked. "You owe me an endless tab for that ride you put us through."

"I'm sorry, sir. Delta cannot accept liability for alcohol. You'll have to buy your own adult beverages." Tucking his electronic tablet underneath his arm, Hall said, "If you will, please follow me." The first officer stepped toward the River Walk with Sharon Henderson on his arm like a date going to the prom.

Kathy watched as the passengers turned and followed. Jayla Watkins walked on ahead, too. Kathy waited to bring up the rear and noticed Dave Einstein turned the opposite way. Before she redirected him, Stinky said:

"Hey, Einstein? Where the heck are you going?"

"I've got an apartment a block away from Jackson Square. I don't need to make a connecting flight. I'll go tomorrow to the airport to file a claim for my luggage."

"For real? You got a place to cool your heels in the French Quarter?"

"My father bought the place for me to live close to Tulane University. I take the streetcar there every day. He plans on selling the apartment when I graduate. He'll make enough in profits for me to have lived there for free."

"Hey, *buddy*," Stinky said with contrived charm in his voice. "I bet you know all the best places to get a drink? I'm talking about where the locals go. Where you get the most bang for your buck."

"Johnny Black's is right by Jackson Square on St. Peter. Most people go to Pat O'leary's, but Johnny Black's sounds like the *hole-in-the-wall* joint you're looking for. It's one of my favorite hangouts," Dave said.

"Since we're going to be stuck here for a while, I don't plan on drinking some high-dollar, watered down drink at a mall. Tell you what, buddy. You show me the way, and I'll buy the first round," Stinky said with the sincerity of a snake oil salesman.

Kathy went to protest with the intent to keep all the passengers together. But Dave didn't need to stay, and Stinky's idea sounded *really* good right now. Especially as she watched Sharon dote over the first officer. If she followed them to the mall, there was no telling what creative things Sharon might find for her to do. Going missing for a couple of hours wouldn't hurt anything. Technically she wasn't on Delta's clock anymore, and she needed to self-medicate in the worst sort of way.

"Hold on," Kathy said as they neared. "I heard you two talking, and I was wondering if you wouldn't mind if I tagged along?"

Dave raised his eyebrows and lower lip. "I don't mind."

"I guess you can come, but I'm not buying you any drinks. The way I see it, you still owe me the drink I wanted on the plane," Stinky said.

"Don't worry, Stinky. I'll buy the first round," Kathy said, realizing the mistake the moment the words left her mouth.

Dave burst out laughing.

Stinky's mouth became a tight O resembling an external sphincter muscle hidden in the nether regions. "Hey! Who are you calling *Stinky*!"

After nearly crashing on landing and watching a dinosaur eat the captain, Kathy wasn't in any mood to take crap from anyone, especially a self-centered passenger. "Well, if the shoe fits, wear it."

*

"We won't get no satisfaction till they tear down Andrew Jackson!"

"We won't get no satisfaction till they tear down Andrew Jackson!"

"We won't get no satisfaction till they tear down Andrew Jackson!"

In the center of Jackson Square, the twenty-thousand-pound Jackson equestrian statue stood high on its granite base. The memorial captured General Jackson's image as he lifts his plumed hat, returning a salute to his troops on the morning of January 8, 1815. His horse is ready to advance, but Jackson restrains it as it balances on its hind legs.

To either side of the commemorative statue memorializing the Battle of New Orleans, protestors faced each other, raising signs, and chanting for their causes.

One side comprised of members of the Alt-Left organization. Each member easily identified by black clothing and concealing headdresses of various designs. These protesters didn't come empty-handed. Everyone had a makeshift weapon of some sort. Chains, hammers, flags on thick wooden poles, and some wore weighted gloves to deliver the mightiest blow in hand-to-hand skirmishes.

The Alt-Left were there to back up Tear Them to the Ground, a group led by Rev. Martin Scott, the key activist leading the cause for removing any historical vestige commemorating white supremacy paid for by tax dollars.

The Alt-Right stood on the opposing side, along with the Sons of the Confederacy, and many unaffiliated citizens in favor of preserving memorials of Southern history. Protest signs, Confederate battle flags, and fists raised in support of keeping the Jackson memorial centerpiece in Jackson Square.

The New Orleans Police Department maintained a visible presence to keep the two sides away from each other. None of the officers wore any riot gear but were quick to get in the face of anyone on either side who attempted to breach civility. Several officers policed from horseback; their shotguns secured in holsters on the horses' sides.

Rev. Scott raised his hands as a cameraman from a local TV station and a reporter approached him. His supporters dialed back the chanting to give their leader a chance to justify their cause.

Surprisingly, the other side stopped their return banter, and the background noise lowered to a minimum.

Rev. Scott removed his cap and ran his hand through his short, graying hair before returning it to the crown of his head. His dark face glistened with sweat, and he righted his shoulders as the reporter stepped up and stuck a microphone toward him.

"Rev. Scott, Jay Weathersby here for WGRZ Eyewitness News. You and your supporters are out in full force today trying to get your message out. Can you tell our viewers why you are here and what Tear Them to the Ground hopes to accomplish?"

"Thank you for the opportunity," Rev. Scott said; the scowl on his face just moments before had melted into a grandfatherly smile. "There is nothing complicated with what we are trying to accomplish. The motive of Tear them to the Ground is to achieve real racial reconciliation. The only true way that can begin is by removing obvious symbols of white supremacy. Our children are born and grow in the shadows of our oppressed history, thus perpetuating the sins of the past. We want to break the chain of inequality. To do this, we must remove taxpayer supported monuments, street names, and public schools named after white supremacists. Then—"

"Then why are you here, Rev. Scott?" a man, who looked to be in his thirties, dressed in a business-casual long sleeve navy blue shirt, gray slacks, and polished shoes yelled from a few feet away on the protestors' side. He held a sign that read: History Is Not Racism.

The reporter shook the microphone the man's way and waved him to come over with the other hand.

Rev. Scott's eyebrows fell, narrowing his gaze.

With a moment of hesitation, the man followed the reporter's beckon and walked over next to Scott.

The reporter asked the man, "The Alt-Right and the Sons of the Confederacy are here today to preserve the statue. Which group do you represent?"

"Neither," he said emphatically. "I'm here because no one has the power to change history. History is a teacher. We should know and preserve our history. And, we should better ourselves based on it."

"That's a tired argument," Rev. Scott said. "These statues are nothing but reminders of history's horrid legacy of white supremacy."

"This statue commemorates Andrew Jackson's role as The Hero of New Orleans. Jackson led five thousand men against fifteen-thousand British soldiers," the man said. "If that doesn't deserve a statue, I don't know what does."

"Jackson murdered thousands of Native Americans and owned over three hundred slaves. If that doesn't depict a white supremacist, I don't know what does," Rev. Scott shot back.

"You cannot use today's moral standards to erase history. We can debate but not without keeping the issues in proper perspective. Jackson's statute is here to commemorate the Battle of New Orleans and for no other reason."

The two sides erupted in opposing jeers and taunts, drowning out any further discussion. Signs, fists, and flags poked at the sky. Police raised their hands to calm the tension.

The reporter pushed the microphone near the man's mouth before he backed away. "Please, sir, can I have your name?"

Looking at the camera and speaking in a loud and clear voice, the man said, "My name is Andrew R. Jackson. I am a descendant of General Andrew Jackson."

*

"I said I was going to buy the first round, and I plan to keep my word," Kathy Stevens said to Dave Einstein, who had told the bartender to set up his friends with whatever they wanted to drink.

She, Stinky (AKA Melvin Posey), and Dave had bellied up to the bar at Johnny Black's. The bar was only half-full. Kathy wondered if that was because of the time of day or if that protest in Jackson Square ran some of the normal business away.

The bartender served the drinks. Dave got a *Parish Rêve*. Stinky got a cocktail called an *Absinthe Frappe*.

Kathy chose another legendary New Orleans libation, the *Sazerac*. The bartender gave a chilled glass a quick rinse of Herbsaint, an anise-flavored liquor, a stiff pour of rye whiskey, sugar, and added Peychaud's bitters.

"I thought you ordered a beer?" Stinky said to Dave. "That looks like coffee."

"It's a style of beer called *stout*. They make this beer in Lafayette with coffee local to the brewery." Dave lifted the mug and sampled his drink.

"What's it taste like?" Stinky asked.

Rolling the stout over his tongue before swallowing, Dave said, "Silky…like sticking your face in a whole bag of coffee beans. Very well balanced…medium mouthfeel. A surprisingly clean finish. Would you like to taste it?"

"Oh, you're one of those craft beer snobs. Figures with your daddy buying you a house in the Quarter. No thanks. If it don't come from Milwaukee, it's not beer," Stinky said.

Dave shrugged his shoulders and pulled out his cellphone, socializing the way Millennials did by ignoring present company in favor of those linked by cell towers.

"What was the drink you ordered again?" Kathy asked Stinky.

Stinky held the tumbler filled with a greenish liquid and cubes of ice. He brought it to his nose and sniffed slowly and deeply.

"This is an absinthe frappe. They outlawed absinthe in the early nineteen hundreds. Absinthe then had wormwood in it, which can cause hallucinations and other mental disorders." He tasted the drink and ran his tongue over his lips. "Interesting...kind of licorice tasting. Smooth...and a little mouth numbing."

"Hopefully it won't numb your mind. You don't need to get s-faced this early in the day. Don't forget we'll have an hour here before we start heading back. You'll want to check in and get your new itinerary," Kathy said and tasted her drink for the first time. Her first impression was mixed. She liked the tang of the sweetened rye whiskey, but the bitters left a slight medicinal taste on her palate.

"Are you always this bossy?" Stinky asked.

"No. I really shine after a few drinks," Kathy said, refusing to let Stinky intimidate her. The previous ordeal of the day had reset her normally accommodating attitude, and she wanted to keep Stinky in his place. He was the type who took a mile if you gave him an inch.

Annoyed, Stinky turned his focus on a TV screen replaying the 2009 SEC Championship Game with the Crimson Tide of Alabama battling the Florida Gators.

Johnny Black's was typical of many small businesses in the French Quarter. Store frontage was a premium, so the bar was eight times deeper than wide. Two sets of narrow double doors were propped open; an invitation to thirsty patrons passing by to stop in and hydrate.

The Sazerac took off some of the edge of the day but didn't bring Kathy to the *happier place* she wanted to go. Well, it *was* only her first drink. She looked at a handwritten menu on a chalkboard for her next selection.

Street noise pushed past the gameday excitement streaming out the TV speakers. Kathy turned on her seat at the bar and looked out the doors open to St. Peter Street.

A young couple ran by, desperately trying not to spill the frozen drinks carried in their hands.

Yells and cries of pain increased in volume as more people dashed past Johnny Black's.

By this time everyone in the bar had their attention diverted to the building turmoil outside.

Stinky's mouth hung open like he was trying to catch flies.

Dave had an eyebrow up and downed the last of his beer.

Kathy thought she felt small tremors shaking the bar.

A ferocious warning in the distance erupted from an unknown creature; sounding something like a love child of a bull elephant and a locomotive.

Some of the patrons ran to the open doors, screamed, and promptly ran to the back of the bar.

Frozen in her chair, Kathy's resolve shattered from the events that happened earlier that day made her legs feel like soggy pasta.

Then, she saw it. The beast plodded in front of a door and raised its head, unleashing another cry. It was as large as a school bus, from what she could tell. Its shape reminded her of a four-legged mammal, most like a rhinoceros, but was brownish-green in color. It had a beak-like mouth, two brow horns set above its eyes, and a smaller horn jutting from its nose. A bony frill fanned the top of its head. One thing for sure, the animal looked like it could burst through a brick wall.

The hair on the nape of Kathy's neck stood on end. This was really happening: the impossible. Just like before when the prehistoric creature took the life of Captain Wesselman, a beast out of time had invaded the present.

"Triceratops...*three horned face*. Interesting," Dave said. Then, he hopped off his bar stool with a phone in hand and attempted to take photographs.

Shockingly, a bum with layers of dirt on his clothing staggered down the middle of the street, holding a bottle wrapped in a brown paper bag in one hand.

"Run away," Kathy said only loud enough for herself to hear. She wanted to scream her warning, but her body would not cooperate. "No!" she managed to say a little louder.

The bum put the bottle to his lips and pointed the bottom to the sky. After a few chugs, he brought it down and wiped his mouth with the back of his hand. A smile widened across his face, and he approached with an outstretched hand with the delight of stroking a miniature horse at a petting zoo.

The triceratops pulled its head back and then thrust it forward. One of the brow horns, over three feet in length, stabbed the bum dead center of his chest.

The bottle fell from his hand and smashed onto the street. He hung limply in the air with blood dripping from front and back, cascading from the triceratops' horn.

Kathy felt more tremors; stronger this time. The pacing was different too, like a creature walking on two legs.

A quick flick of its head and the triceratops slung the bum to the side, and directly in one of Johnny Black's doorways.

People screamed so loudly that Kathy thought her ears would burst. She noticed Stinky had finished his drink and waved to hail the attention of the bartender for another. Never had she encountered such a selfish individual. What made that man tick?

The triceratops brayed once again, and what she could only describe as a thunderous, reptilian hiss, fired back. There was no doubt the ground shook now, and the reason why became obvious when a new dinosaur entered the scene.

The dinosaur resembled a bipedal lizard. It was over fifteen feet tall, and counting the tail, almost twice as long. It had grayish skin with darker stripes running from its spine down its side. Two small arms bounced in front of its chest, and the tail shifted to balance its body on powerful looking legs. Even Kathy knew a T. rex when she saw one.

A T. rex...in New Orleans. What is the world coming to?

The T. rex opened its monstrous mouth, showing rows of sharp, jagged teeth, and hissed again.

The sheer mass of the two dinosaurs astounded her. The triceratops didn't stand as tall as the T. rex, but it was noticeably longer. And even though the triceratops didn't have teeth, its beak looked powerful enough to chomp the rex's leg in two with one bite.

The T. rex dipped its head forward and shifted its body about, threatening to attack.

Holding its ground, the triceratops brayed loudly. It lifted its head and pointed its brow horns at the rex.

The death dance began with the T. rex stepping toward the tetrapod and biting empty air near its head. The brow horns narrowly missed the rex's mouth, and the animal stepped back in retreat.

Trying to get a rear advantage, the rex attempted to circle the triceratops.

The tetrapod had no problem getting outflanked; especially with Pat O'Leary's acting as a wall on that side of the street. It spun on its five-toed feet to keep its armored head pointed at the predator.

The rex lunged, but its jaws didn't connect. The triceratops drove its head forward, digging its horns into the rex's gut, and backing it into O'Leary's façade.

With its small arms flailing, the rex thrashed its head and twisted its body enough to wiggle free. Red blood oozed down its stomach where the horns had pushed two gaping holes.

The savagery of the situation had numbed Johnny Black's patrons to silence. Kathy could hardly breathe from the firm hand of fear's grip. For a moment, she thought the rex might be on the retreat, but the creature's ire had it on the attack again.

The T. rex extended its mighty jaws for the triceratops' head. Spikey teeth chomped on one of the brow horns. The triceratops struggled to pull free. The rex didn't waver and held fast through the cries of its victim, twisting its head until the horn snapped in half.

Backing away, the triceratops kept its head up, warning the rex it still had plenty of fight left in it.

No matter. The rex dove with another crushing bite that came down on one side of the prey's frill. Sharp snaps of breaking bone penetrated the brays of the tetrapod.

Hissing a battle cry, the rex lunged for another bite.

The triceratops twisted its head to the side to avoid the sharp teeth, leaving the back of its neck vulnerable.

The rex's jaws opened wide and bit behind the frill. Blood squirted like a tomato smashed with a sledge hammer.

Kathy's bowels rattled at the triceratops' death-cry. She had to remind herself to breathe.

The T. rex's jaws held firm. It then twisted its head from side to side until the tetrapod fell to its knees and laid on its side.

Pulling back, the rex came away with a chunk of blood-dripping meat. It threw its head back and worked its jaws until the mouthful traveled down its throat and into its belly.

Undeterred by its foreign surroundings, the T. rex went back to satiate its hunger.

Dave returned from a window with a content grin on his face. "Can you believe your very own eyes! We have witnessed an event no other human has."

Terror's grip had loosened enough for Kathy to move again. She understood Dave's excitement. That was fine and good as long as the humans remained spectators and not participants.

She turned her gaze over and saw Stinky's empty bar stool. Looking up, Kathy saw he had climbed over the bar and was in the process of preparing himself an obscenely large cocktail, with a bottle of liquor in each hand topping it off.

Stinky saw her giving him the evil eye. "Never let a crisis go to waste," he said unapologetically.

The bartender had abandoned his station and had probably left out a rear entrance. Stinky was the kind who was going to make sure he got his, and everyone else needed to worry about themselves. His selfishness knew no boundaries.

Kathy turned back to Dave, and said, "Make that *two* events no other humans have ever witnessed." She stuck a thumb over her shoulder and directed it toward Stinky.

Dave looked over and shook his head in disgust.

CHAPTER 5

The news reporter had left Jackson Square not long before tensions escalated. The gap between the two opposing sides now nonexistent.

Grossly outnumbered, the police had retreated and gathered in small groups. Andrew heard one officer, as he hurried by, call on his radio for backup.

Rev. Martin Scott, the leader of Tear Them to the Ground, was in the face of one member of the Sons of the Confederacy.

Andrew Jackson was so hoping that this would have remained a civil protest. Extreme right and left positions on any subject had obvious flaws. There had to be bending on both sides if differences had any hope of a resolution. The only way *winner could take all* was if one side obliterated the other. America didn't need another Civil War.

Rev. Scott threw his protest sign to the ground and put up his fists, ready to defend himself.

The Sons of Confederacy member in front of him had thrown his sign aside first. Andrew quickly grabbed the man's right arm to prevent blows from flying.

The man outweighed Andrew by a good forty pounds. And while it was a valiant effort to keep the peace, the man jerked free of Andrew's grip, and his fist accidentally flew forward landing square in the middle of Scott's face.

Rev. Scott, old age limited and taken aback by a sucker punch, staggered to the ground.

One ardent supporter immediately took Scott's spot, and said, "You goin' down, fool!"

The two exchanged blows, igniting the *mêlée*.

The police responded by blowing whistles and yelling warnings over megaphones.

Signs and fists became weapons. Makeshift weapons clashed as the protest turned into a full-scale war.

Andrew, unarmed with no intention of fighting, backed away as chains swung and blunt instruments struck flesh. There was no doubt that people would get hurt. Some might even receive life-threatening injuries. Today, both sides of the argument would lose.

Outside the mass of people in the center of Jackson Square, a mounted police officer had his shotgun to his shoulder and squeezed off three rounds.

Pandemonium dialed upward tenfold. The situation had turned beyond horrific. What had possessed the officer to fire a gun?

Then, more gunshots rang out from different corners of the square.

The gunfire induced a momentary pause as warring sides looked around for a greater threat than what was before them.

Andrew watched as people in the outside region of the group screamed and dashed away. Catching brief glances between those who fled, he saw a strange looking two-legged creature.

At first, he thought it might be someone pulling a stunt. That notion quickly dissipated when he watched it chase a full-grown man and take him down to the ground.

The creature looked like a dinosaur. *A dinosaur? Impossible!* It had a lizard-like head with large eyes. When it opened its mouth, it had rows of leaf-shaped teeth. Long, slender legs with raised sickle-shaped claws on the inside of its feet looked like they could have belonged on a bird. The head and body were reptilian, though, stretching at least six feet in length, and over three feet in height. Its olive-green skin had golden stripes marking its spine.

The dinosaur wasn't as tall as a human, but size, in this case, didn't matter. It bit the back of the man's neck until he gave up all efforts to resist.

The troodon's hunger overrode any fear of the large crowd around it. It began stripping flesh above the man's left elbow. A flap of meat hung from its lower jaw and stained it red as it gobbled it down.

Andrew felt his insides churning and fought to keep his stomach contents in place.

Alt-Left and Alt-Right duelers, who previously battled to take the other out, teamed up on the dinosaur. One had a chain in his right hand and a hammer in his left. The second held a large diameter flagpole that easily could second as a *hanbō* in a martial arts match.

While the troodon's head lowered for another bite, the man with the chain slung it forward. The chain was long enough to where when it hit the dinosaur's neck, it wrapped around it a couple of times.

Startled, the troodon jerked its head backward.

To the chain-wielder's misfortune, he had the other end wrapped around his right hand. The troodon pulled him off balance, and he landed flat on his face on top of the dead man.

The troodon snaked its head around until the chain pulled free.

Cursing, the man rolled on his back and saw the reptile-like jaws open and deadly, bloodstained teeth plunging toward him.

The man with the pole bounded forward just in time to shove the pole between the troodon's teeth, split-seconds before reaching its target.

The troodon raised its head and hissed in anger. It tried to shake the pole from its mouth, but its teeth had stuck in the wood.

The pole wielder cried out as he struggled with the dinosaur. His arms shook as he put every ounce of muscle to keep the dinosaur at bay.

In the blink of an eye, the troodon leaped forward bringing the sickle-shaped foot claws down on the man's stomach. Clothing and flesh ripped, and a gush of crimson spewed out.

The man dropped the pole and screamed in anguish as he held his hands on his gaping wound; desparetly trying to keep his intestines from spilling out.

From behind, a rope turned into a lasso landed around the troodon's neck.

"Got 'em. Let's pull, boys!" a member of the Sons of Confederacy yelled.

The troodon went to its back. As the Alt-Right members held tightly, the Alt-Left members pounded the deadly creature with bricks and clubs. Some even stuck it with knives until it became a bleeding, unmoving heap.

Andrew felt naked with nothing in his hands to defend himself. He looked around in hope to find something that could put distance between him and one of those dinosaurs. There was road construction nearby where he earlier saw lengths of rebar that would make a formidable spear, but that was just outside of the fence and too far away.

Then Andrew saw Rev. Scott trying to lift himself off the ground. There were footprints on his shirt. People running in fear must have stepped on the old guy.

He dashed over to Scott's side, keeping one eye out for another attack. "Hey, you okay? Let me help you up."

Dazed, but coming out of it, Rev. Scott raised his right arm, and Andrew pulled him to his feet.

"Ow! My knee. Somebody stepped on my right knee," Scott cried and gritted his teeth.

"Sorry, buddy. Here, put your arm around me, and take the weight off that leg."

It may be true that there are no Atheists in foxholes. It was true too that the enemy of my enemy is my friend.

Andrew looked for a place of refuge to bring Rev. Scott. Before him stood the mighty bronze statue of General Andrew Jackson. St. Louis Cathedral, the oldest Catholic cathedral in daily use, just outside of the Square, and across Chartres Street, loomed in the background. The beautiful white building had served parishioners since 1794. Its triple steeples towered like welcoming arms, ready to comfort the poor souls in need.

"I'm taking you to the cathedral. Let's go!" Andrew said, and the two hobbled toward the nearest gate.

Scott winced in pain with each step, but the man soldiered on.

From Andrew's assessment, half the protestors fled the scene, and the other half willingly or unwillingly engaged with more dinosaurs. Some protestors weren't fairing so well. Horrible death screams electrified the air sending chills down his spine. He was so scared he couldn't feel his legs, but he kept telling them to keep churning.

At least there weren't any dinosaurs of the magnitude of those in Jurassic Park. The movies had fascinated him when he first saw them and thought how wonderful it would be if man could bring the prehistoric creatures back. Behind bars, though. Humans had no chance of competing with dinosaurs in the wild.

A savage roar lit a fire under the fleeing men's feet right after they passed the General Jackson statue.

Andrew had counted his blessings too soon. He looked over his shoulder and saw a two-legged dinosaur as tall as the General Jackson memorial. The creature's head was at least six feet long. It looked similar to drawings of T. rex's he'd seen, but the size and shape of it made him think Godzilla and a T. rex had crossed and out came that guy.

The dinosaur's belly was off-white. The skin on its back was a light tan. Dark brown spots that reminded Andrew of a giraffe dotted near its spine. It was beautifully terrifying.

How could a creature of that size come from nowhere?

Fortunately, it had fixated its attention on the General's statue; perhaps seeing something as large as it as a threat. It roared again and slammed its head and body into the sculpted metal.

The giganotosaurus did what the Civil War, time, and hurricanes over the last one hundred and seventy years could not. The famous equestrian statue dislodged from its granite base, and the force of it hitting the ground broke the twenty-thousand-pound memorial into large pieces.

It was indeed a sad day in history for losing such a treasure.

The day wasn't over, and history might have worse things to record at the conclusion.

*

Officer Charles Tidwell leaned back in his saddle, rubbed the small of his back, and wished the mayor would have requested fifty or more members of the Louisiana National Guard to maintain order at the protest.

Sergeant Darryl Ginyard was on his radio now, calling for backup.

There was a time when people respected the law. Just the presence of one police officer in a situation like this would have kept events from getting out of hand. Now, even five of the eleven of the iconic New Orleans Police Department's Mounted Unit, and a handful of other officers, were no more of a deterrent than pigeons foraging in the Square.

Tidwell had seen the worst men had to offer over the last twenty-five years of his career. Hurricane Katrina, back in 2005, had him almost finding his breaking point. The sad fact then was some of the NOPD turned out to be worse than the most hardened criminals ever to emerge from the Crescent City.

He had stuck it out, though. Reaching deep inside and finding a resolve he never knew. That was then when he was younger. The long hours, the stress of the job, and the growing anarchy in the United States made him feel twice as old as then. Fortunately, retirement hung like a brass ring on a merry-go-round just a few months away.

Sergeant Ginyard spoke on his radio, listened to the noisy response, and said to Tidwell, "Just got word the governor has approved the deployment of three squads of National Guard."

"Three squads? Having thirty extra guys on our side might turn things around here. Should have been here this morning," Tidwell said, wondering why politicians only acted to put out fires rather than prevent them from happening.

"Yeah, looks like this thing is about to boil over. We're going to crack a few heads for sure. Try to keep the numbers even. We don't want to *set straight* one side more than the other."

"Wouldn't want to be called *racists*," Tidwell said.

The two men laughed together.

"Funny how both a white man like me and a black man like you could both be called racists in this situation," Tidwell said. This new politically correct world had shifted the zeitgeist in the US where *up means down* and *left means right* as far as Tidwell was concerned. Of course, if he headed over to Cafe du Monde for beignets and chicory coffee right now to find his *safe space*, the snowflake Millennials would have zero compassion for him.

"When I wear this uniform, I'm not black, I'm blue," Ginyard said. "And, I don't care about the color of the skin of whose head I crack."

"That's why you and I get along so well. We're so much alike," Tidwell said adding a wink and a nod.

Then, without warning, Tidwell pulled his shotgun from its holster and brought it to his shoulder. The barrel pointed directly at Sergeant Ginyard's face. He yelled, "Down, Ginyard! Move!"

Ginyard's face went blank only for a microsecond. Then, he did as commanded and flattened to the ground.

No sooner had Ginyard unimpeded the shotgun's aim, Tidwell pumped three rounds as fast as he could into a monstrosity only seconds away from sinking its teeth into Sergeant Ginyard. That darn thing had come from nowhere!

The creature looked similar to the green Carolina anole lizard. That green lizard only grew up to six inches or so, though. This aberration's body was nearly six feet long, with a tail adding another three feet. Where it differed the most from a common lizard, the thing had a five-foot-sail-like fin on its back. The fin rose as high in the air as Tidwell seated on his horse. Its head was more iguana-ish and had rows of teeth that would spook the largest gator.

Call it luck, or call it twenty-five years of training paying off, the double ought buckshot traveled a tight three-inch spread until it reached dead center of its target.

The dimetrodon's face imploded on one side of its head; leaving a crater of fresh ground meat. The dinosaur dropped on all fours and listed over to its side.

The warring factions amped their game in response to the shots.

To confuse the situation more, other gunshots rang from around the Square. Tidwell hoped those rounds came from other police officers. Although, he was just starting to wrap his mind around what had just happened there, he realized others might have found themselves in the same predicament. What on Earth was going on?

The dead creature lying just a few yards away looked just like one of those plastic dinosaurs he played with as a kid. Tidwell couldn't remember its official name. He just called it *Donnie* because it was easier to pronounce. He hoped he wouldn't get a modern-day encounter from *Terry* or *Rexy*.

"What the heck is that?" Sergeant Ginyard said as he scrambled to his feet with his Glock .40 caliber service pistol drawn and pointing at the dimetrodon. "Is it dead?"

The beast's remaining eye was open and looking into an unseen void. Because it showed no signs of movement or life, Tidwell declared victory. "Looks dead to me."

Victory was short-lived. Just on the other side of the fence, where the mule-drawn carriages waited to take those who desired a tour of the city, a thunderous hiss overshadowed an almost human-like scream from a mule.

Tidwell spun around in his saddle and saw a two-legged dinosaur over twelve feet tall, with its jaws in a death-grip around the mule's throat.

The carriage driver stood in his seat, slapping the top of the dinosaur's head with his riding crop. "Hey! Whoa! Stop! Stop!"

No sooner as the mule collapsed, the allosaurus' open mouth went after its interrogator, which it quickly filled with his head and torso. Its teeth mashed together as the carriage driver's legs kicked in the empty air.

Sergeant Ginyard bounded toward the fray, and Tidwell pulled the reins on his horse, *New Orleans Lady*. He passed Ginyard before the sergeant made it to the gate leading to Decatur Street, where the carriages lined up.

The carriage driver behind the one attacked wasted no time in bugging out before he became the next course of the dinosaur's meal. He veered in front of oncoming traffic, where a car had to choose a light pole instead of hitting the mule. The vehicle smashed into the immovable object to the sound of metal crunching and glass breaking. Steam billowed out from underneath its hood.

No time to check on the driver, Tidwell held his shotgun in one hand while guiding his faithful steed with the other. The other carriages sped away from the dinosaur, but traffic slowed to a standstill now that the behemoth and crashed car blocked the way. Drivers coming to a stop thought it best to abandon on foot and quickly dashed from their cars. Some ran in the opposite direction, while others took the steps leading up to the Washington Artillery Park memorial.

Tidwell expected people to scatter out of sight, but to his dismay, he noticed many chose to sit on the steps as if they were watching the New Orleans Saints playing football.

The allosaurus looked like a smaller version of a T. rex but none less deadly. The only thing left of the carriage driver were two boots laying on the ground. His legs cut just below his knees and leaking red on the cobblestone street.

As Tidwell approached, the dinosaur must have heard the horseshoes clopping on stone. It turned its beady eyes on him. For some reason, the allosaurus' eyes reminded him of a shark's before it rolled them to the back of its head when attacking its victim.

The allosaurus stomped toward him.

New Orleans Lady was one of the finest animals Tidwell had ever ridden. The poor girl had never encountered pheromones from prehistoric times before, and when they hit her nostrils, it sent her back on her heels.

For a moment, Tidwell thought he would spill off the horse's back and eat cobblestone. By a miracle, he managed to hang on and dug his heels into Lady's side to calm her down. He dropped the reins and brought the shotgun up to his side. He pumped three more shells through the barrel and into the allosaurus' chest.

The blasts stopped the dinosaur's advance but didn't bring it to its knees. Why should it have? The ammo was designed to stop deer and other wild game, not dinosaurs. Dinosaurs! How in the heck were dinosaurs on the loose in New Orleans? Slugs in his saddlebag might be more effective than the nine pellet double-aught buckshot, but he had no time to reload. In fact, there was only one shell left in his shotgun. If that shell didn't make the kill, he hoped Lady could get them out of there before he smelled dinosaur breath.

Sergeant Ginyard raced alongside and unloaded a magazine from his .40.

Lady attempted to throw Tidwell again. He couldn't be of any help if he found himself on his butt, so he quickly dismounted and slapped Lady on the rear. She ran off with her bristles riding high on her back.

Tidwell couldn't blame her. His lower colon felt like a rag flapping in hurricane winds, but he had to harden the center of his core and keep it together. Dropping the shotgun, he pulled out his pistol and let lead fly while Ginyard reloaded. At least the bullets were hurting or confusing the beast enough to keep it from charging.

Ginyard reloaded and snapped one in the chamber as Tidwell's slide locked back. The two stepped out from in front of the allosaurus, putting the carriage between it and themselves.

The throaty bark of off-road vehicles encroached the chaos swirling around Jackson Square.

Tidwell immediately recognized the familiar sound as another unlawful visit from the *Bywater Boyz* to the French Quarter. The gang was infamous for invading the major tourist area during broad daylight. Dirt bikes roared down narrow streets, weaving in and out of traffic, popping wheelies and other stunts. Four wheelers joined in, creating a commuter nightmare.

Law enforcement endangered more people when trying to bring the violators to justice. So, the policy in place let the revelers have the road and hope they would leave before harming anyone. The Bywater Boyz picked a bad day to show their asses.

"How do we kill this thing?" Ginyard shouted and fired.

"I don't know that we can," Tidwell said, having no more of an idea how to get out of this mess than how they got into it.

Ginyard's slide locked open. "I'm out!"

Sensing advantage, the allosaurus lunged forward, pushing the side of the carriage up on its side and turned it over.

The two officers dodged in opposite directions to avoid the carriage. Unfortunately, the rear of the carriage landed on top of Ginyard.

Tidwell stumbled off balance and fell on his right elbow, tearing a nice hole in his shirtsleeve and leaving skin on the sidewalk. While on his back, he took careful aim and tried to make the rest of his bullets count.

The allosaurus saw the trapped human as the weakest of the herd and went in for the kill.

The symphony of un-muffled exhaust from the Bywater Boyz' off-road vehicles did nothing to distract the dinosaur's killer instinct.

With no time to spare, Tidwell had one last attempt to save his brother in blue and friend. He sprang to his feet and ran over to the shotgun laying in the street. Pumping the last shell in the chamber, he ran and placed the barrel directly against the allosaurus' left leg and pulled the trigger.

It truly had sounded as if the theropod screamed.

The next thing Tidwell knew, he was sent flying backward and sliding down the street. He came to a halt, dazed, and tried to focus his eyes.

He had managed to turn the dinosaur's attention to himself and was completely out of options of what to do next.

Two ATVs with masked riders rolled up next to Ginyard. Both dismounted and lifted the carriage off of the sergeant, who pulled his trapped leg from underneath.

The allosaurus was content to let one victim go. Tidwell had brought it pain and needed to make amends by giving up his life.

Three dirt bikes flying the Bywater Boyz' colors rumbled up the street and cut between the distance of Tidwell and dinosaur. They started blowing their horns and running circles around the allosaurus.

The dinosaur stopped cold and raised its arms in confusion. Then it bit into empty air as it attempted to grab the evading riders.

Another dirt bike skidded up and turned one hundred eighty degrees, the rear tire coming to a stop right next to Tidwell's head. "Get up and get on!" the rider commanded.

Tidwell saw Ginyard hop a ride on one of the ATVs and head off away from the allosaurus as he got to his feet. The rider slid forward, and he eagerly jumped on the seat.

The rider goosed the throttle. The front wheel left the road, and the rider yelled out a victory cry.

The other dirt bikes peeled away from the dinosaur and followed.

Tidwell had his arms wrapped around an outlaw that saved his life. One of law enforcements' greatest nemeses became his savior. *The irony of it all.*

He glanced to his right just as they passed one of the street artists who had chosen to watch the battle. The artist drew a caricature of the allosaurus tangling with the two officers etched on white paper in charcoal.

Even in the most tragic of events, New Orleanians' *let the good times roll.*

CHAPTER 6

Dr. Bryan Breaux felt the beaming rays of the sun heat his sweaty forehead as he and Bridget Reed stood on the roof of Pat O'Leary's. His head buzzed like a hornet's nest from a combination of cheap rum and the impossible situation he found himself in. A situation he had created when the particle entanglement experiment created a consequence he had never considered.

Pat O's patio below him was a mass of chaos. Prehistoric dinosaurs ran amuck attacking defenseless patrons. Killing was truly as easy as shooting fish in a barrel.

Partially eaten bodies lay about on the floor. Some with entrails pulled from the bodies and strewn across the dark slate. More than one victim showed signs of life; twitching, jerking, and others moaned in great agony.

All the exits must have been blocked. Hopelessness weighed on Breaux's soul like a thousand pound weight.

"Dr. Breaux?" Bridget said.

He heard his student but couldn't find the will to answer.

"Dr. Breaux! Coming up the street…it's another dinosaur."

The news added more despair. Turning his gaze, he saw a brownish-green triceratops roll up St. Peter Street. People scattered from its path in a frenzied escape.

The triceratops acted as if it felt as out of place as it looked. It roared and turned its head from side to side as if searching for a way out of the concrete jungle.

"That thing is huge," Bridget said. "Something that size can tear up the whole city."

People from the bar *Johnny Black's* from across the street came outside to get a glimpse. A couple who ran past the bar, protecting their drinks from spilling as if it were equal to saving their lives, epitomized the *Big Eazy* lifestyle.

The triceratops came to a stop right in front of Bridget and Breaux and roared again.

The professor marveled at the size of the beast. Its beak-like mouth didn't seem like it belonged on the four-legged body.

What was it going to take to corral this thing and get it out of there? Where would it be brought to or what could contain it? It would take an M1 Abrams tank to take the dinosaur down. What then? Butcher it in place and have a barbeque?

When a bum pulled himself off the sidewalk and staggered toward the triceratops, Breaux was so numb he couldn't even speak.

"Hey! Get away from that thing. Run!" Bridget yelled down.

It wasn't a shock when the three-foot brow horn skewered the bum in the chest. In fact, Breaux expected no less.

What he didn't expect was the T. rex who came down the street to challenge the triceratops.

The ground shook. The two beasts hissed and roared their intentions, bringing on the battle.

Breaux melted to his knees as the clash of the Titans began, and then laid on his side and curled in the fetal position.

Bridget had hit the deck too because the warring giants were right out front of them.

*

Time seemed to stand still during the lashing and thrashing. Breaux felt as if his spirit had left his body and floated in a Sargasso Sea in another dimension. His will to live ebbed. Breathing became more of an effort than he could afford.

*

"Wake up, Doc," Bridget said while nudging the professor.

The professor's eyes were wide open as was his mouth, but he was unresponsive.

"Doc, wake up." She grabbed his shoulder this time and gave it a shake.

Breaux's head moved about like a noodle connected it to his body.

Is he even breathing? she thought. "Doc!" Bridget said louder than she had intended, bringing an open hand down on his cheek. The ensuing *slap* sounded louder than when she last called his name.

Breaux's dilated pupils shrank to normal size. He made a sound just short of a gasp. Closing his mouth, he cleared his throat, and said, "I don't want to die. I've been given a second chance to live. I don't want to die."

"Good. I don't want to die either. We've got to survive this thing so you can give me an A for the semester," Bridget said; her response intended to be more sarcastic than humorous. This was no time for the professor to check out. His ass needed to be *on*, and she didn't have time to deal with the threats the new world had to offer and lug him around too.

Bridget and Breaux climbed to their hands and knees and peered over the side of the roof to the street below.

The T. rex had won the battle and took the time to fatten its belly with the spoils of war before leaving down St. Peter toward Jackson Square.

The triceratops was directly below them. A good portion of the neck and shoulder on the exposed side had been eaten. Bridget was a little surprised to see the blood and meat looked so much like the pigs she'd seen slaughtered.

Growing up, her granddaddy used to raise and butcher his own pigs. Her granddaddy used to cook *Everything but the squeal*, as he would say. Her favorite part of the pig was the fried skin called *cracklins*. She doubted her teeth could cut through fried triceratops skin.

"We've got to get down from here, Doc."

Breaux looked over to her, his eyelids half-open. "Why? We're safe up here."

"I don't know how much longer that will last," Bridget said. "Look to your left and up."

The professor did as he was told, closing one eye and his chin dropping. "A pterosaur of some type. Like the one we saw earlier."

"Yeah, only about thirty times bigger. If that thing sees us, it will come down here and eat us just as easy as that little one ate that lizard. I don't know about you, but I'm not willing to become bird food."

Bridget didn't mention she also wanted to get away from the ongoing carnage behind them at Pat O's. She didn't think a dinosaur below could figure out a way to climb on the roof like they had, but she didn't want to stick around and find out. "We're going to have to jump."

"But it's almost twenty feet down to hard concrete. We're likely to break a bone and then we won't be able to run anymore. Something will get us…" the professor's words drifted, and he turned his gaze back to the blood feast on the patio.

"That overgrown, horned pig is right underneath. I don't think it's as soft as a pillow, but it's made of meat. I think it'll absorb enough impact that we'll be okay. Plus, that lump is probably eight feet high. The fall won't be as far."

The professor stared blankly over at the triceratops. "I don't know…"

Oh hell, no. This was no time for Doc Breaux to become a liability. "Well, *I do know.* Get that skinny white ass up, and get over here," Bridget said, not waiting for a response as she rose. It wasn't a question she asked; it was a demand she made.

Stepping a few feet over to target her landing site, she said, "Get up. NOW!"

The professor picked one leg up and put his foot on the roof and then slowly followed with the other.

"I'll go first," Bridget said. Gazing down, she hoped there was a good layer of meat and fat on the triceratops' ribs. Plus, she wanted to avoid the bloody exposed meat from where the rex ate its lunch.

It had been a while since she'd jumped from something that high. As kids, she and her cousins would get on her granddaddy's barn and jump onto stacks of hay.

Her feet solidly landed on the fallen dinosaur, and she reached out her hands and dropped to her knees to stabilize herself. *That wasn't too bad.*

Flipping around, with her bottom resting on the beast, she slid to the sidewalk. The impact from that drop was a bit more jarring than when she had jumped from the roof, but she was okay. *Yuk.* Except that her left hand had come in contact with blood. She almost wiped her hand on her pants but then looked around for something else to clean it on.

"Are you okay?" the professor asked.

"I'm fine. Just do like I did. Don't think about it too much. Just do it and get it over with."

Dr. Breaux closed his eyes, but before he jumped, he opened them again.

He landed with the grace of a rag-doll but at least appeared unhurt. Not bothering to turn, he let his feet dangle and slowly slid down the side and stomach of the beast until dropping to the sidewalk.

"You're okay, right?" Bridget asked while holding her left hand out away from her side.

"I am uninjured," Breaux said and adjusted his shirt collar. He looked up and down the street. "Where to now?"

Bridget checked the sky again and saw a few more pterosaurs had come over uninvited. They were far away enough not to be a current threat. "We need to find someplace safe—where we can hide out for a while. It'd be nice to have some water and food too."

"Johnny Black's is right across the street. They'll at least have water."

No sooner had the professor spoken, than two men and a woman bolted from Johnny Black's.

The woman turned her gaze toward her, and then shouted, "Run!"

*

Kathy Stevens and Dave Einstein stared daggers at Stinky (Melvin Posey) as he shook the last few drops out of a liquor bottle into a forty-eight-ounce plastic cup.

A triceratops had just battled it out with a T. rex right outside of Johnny Black's and came up short in the fight. The other patrons fled out the back in fear of losing their lives.

Dave and Kathy had stayed and watched in fascination at the unique event.

Stinky was the only one who was more concerned with helping himself to a free drink than the threat of danger. This in no way was a gauge of his bravery. Instead, it was a badge of his self-absorbed gluttony.

Stinky's raised eyebrows and mischievous smirk let the onlookers know he was quite proud of himself. He stirred his concoction with a straw and licked it clean. He turned his gaze to the ceiling and pursed his lips, and then said, "Hmm, needs a squeeze of lemon." After mashing a wedge of lemon with his fingers above his drink, he said, "And cherries. I like cherries." Plucking a few of the bright red fruits from the drink station tray, he placed them on top and stirred again with the straw.

"If you drink that you won't be able to walk out of here," Kathy said.

Stinky's cheeks collapsed as he sucked deeply from the straw. After a few gulps, he stuck his tongue out and smiled big enough to show gritted teeth. "That's strong," he said as if to himself. He turned his gaze to Kathy. "I'm not going to drink all of this here. It's a *to-go* cup."

Kathy looked over at Dave. "Everyone else left out the back door. I wonder where they all went."

"The back leads to a street called *Pirate Alley*," Dave said.

"Why is it called Pirate Alley?" Stinky asked.

"A few reasons, as the legends go. There used to be a jail that housed pirates on that street. The most interesting story was that the pirate Jean Lafitte and Andrew Jackson met there where they formed the unlikely alliance that led to the defeat of the British at the Battle of New Orleans. Pirates had become patriots after the war, and the name Pirate Alley stuck," Dave said.

"What's down Pirate Alley now?" Kathy asked.

"Not much. A café, a bar, a mask shop. The other side of the alley is an iron fence surrounding St. Anthony's Garden," Dave said.

"Well, we can't stay here. Those bifold doors in the front have chains with locks keeping us from closing them. They don't look very sturdy anyway," Kathy said.

"If we leave out the back, we might make it over to my place. It's a few streets over and a block or two toward the river," Dave said.

"Sounds like a plan," Kathy said. "Are you coming with us?" she asked Stinky.

Frowning, the man said, "Why wouldn't I? We're a team."

"You're a team of *one*," Kathy said, holding back a few other sentiments. Before Stinky had a chance at rebuttal, she said, "Get your ass in gear and let's go."

Leading the way, Kathy felt light-headed as she stepped toward the rear. Maybe that one drink she drank had more of a punch than she originally thought.

Stinky pulled himself up, planted his butt on the bar, and then bailed off onto the other side. He reached and grabbed his cup, fueling up with a couple of gulps before tagging behind Dave and Kathy.

The rear doors' sign read, ALARM WILL SOUND WHEN OPENED. Of course, no alarm had gone off earlier, so there was no reason to worry about that now.

Kathy waited for Stinky's arrival, but Dave walked past her.

The rear doors resembled two large barn doors. Dave slowly opened the nearest door. He looked out to the right and then turned his head to the left.

A horrible shriek from outside sent Kathy back against the wall.

Dave jerked his head inside and closed the door so fast it bumped his forehead.

"What was that?" Kathy asked, her hand over her heart.

Dave stood partially frozen, his fists hovering above his chest. Taking a deep breath, he said in a shaky voice, "I...think it was a *Utahraptor*."

"Utah-rapper?" Stinky said.

"U-tah-rap-tor," Dave said.

"Utah like the state *Utah*?" Stinky asked.

"Yes."

"Why'd they call it Utahraptor? Because it had multiple wives or something like that?" Stinky asked.

Dave closed his eyes and his chest deflated. "No, you *simpleton*." His words had seethed from his lips. Gaining his composure, he said, "They named it that because the first fossils were found in Utah—back around nineteen seventy-five, I think."

This was the first time Kathy had seen the young man show emotion. So far he acted as if he was a wandering observer in life where nothing on the outside affected him. "That thing scared you, didn't it?"

Dave nodded and cautiously chuckled. "Yeah, it did at that. It was so close. I know I only got a glimpse of it, but..." He rubbed his chin. "It's big—tall as a man, but its body is over twice as long as it stands. The Utahraptor has bird characteristics, with short arms covered with feathers and a long feathered tail. I didn't have time to look at its claws. I know fossils they've found have claws measuring twenty-four centimeters."

"How long is that in *American*?" Stinky asked.

"Over nine inches," Dave said. "I did get to see its teeth. Each tooth was bigger than my thumb."

Stinky held his thumb up and looked at it. "That's some pretty big choppers, right there."

The Utahraptor cried right outside the doors.

Kathy and Dave both jumped.

Stinky stopped mid-suck on his straw.

The raptor hit the doors, which seemed to momentarily buckle inward.

Kathy saw the fear on Dave's face and thought she was looking in a mirror.

The doors were pounded upon again, and a black claw poked through splintering wood near midway.

"These doors must be almost a hundred years old. The Utahraptor will punch through them like they're cardboard," Dave said.

No one had to tell Kathy twice. "Stinky, move it out of here!"

Fortunately, Stinky pushed his obstination aside and led the way; maintaining a two-hand grip on his drink.

Dave followed on his heels.

Wood cracked then crackled. The Utahraptor was busting through!

Just as Kathy followed Dave outside, she saw a young black woman and an older white man standing near the triceratops. She only had enough extra breath to yell, "Run!"

CHAPTER 7

T-Bob Buche had been working at the Audubon Zoo for the last fifteen years. Getting a job there wasn't easy for someone in his circumstance. His mother had to go through the state to petition the Audubon Nature Institute to allow a special needs adult the opportunity.

The Institute didn't *give* T-Bob the position. He had to earn it—had to prove to be capable of taking orders, performing tasks, and care properly for the animals. That was no problem for him. The years of remedial schooling to help him adjust to a world that ticked at a pace just a little too fast had prepared him well. It didn't hurt that he had a deep passion for caring for animals.

In fact, if anyone were to ask him his honest feelings, he'd say that he preferred animals to people. People could be mean; not like a scared animal who was only trying to protect itself. People had treated him awful—making fun of the way he looked and when he just didn't understand why they didn't want to be his friends.

"Excuse me. Can you tell us where the dinosaur exhibit is? I have an old map, and it doesn't show it," a man built to play linebacker for the New Orleans Saints asked. He stood next to a pretty woman notably shorter than him. The woman held the hand of a cute girl probably not older than ten. The girl's long braids cascaded down her back.

"Hello, my name is T-Bob. You sure picked a nice day to come to the zoo."

"Yeah. I'm glad there's no chance of rain today. I don't get many days off with my job," the man said.

"You don't have to work as much as you do. You *chose* to work all of that overtime," the woman said and then tightened her lips and stared at the man.

The man looked down at the sidewalk and shook his head; obviously holding back a defense. He looked up at T-Bob, and said, "We took a riverboat up here. My daughter's been dying to see the new dinosaur exhibit. Which is…?"

"Oh, that's not far from where we are. Just follow that sidewalk and stay left," T-Bob said and pointed. "You'll come up to a new sign that'll tell you right where to go."

"Thanks," the man said.

T-Bob lowered his head toward the little girl. "Hello, my name is T-Bob. My dad's name is Bob, so they called me T-Bob. You know, because I was *little* Bob when I was born. What's your name?"

The little girl's eyes brightened. "My name is Keesha. *Keesha* means *great joy*," she said matter-of-factly.

"You sound like a smart girl. Your dad says you like dinosaurs. What's your favorite dinosaur?" T-Bob asked.

"I like the brontosaurus because they were nice dinosaurs. They ate leaves and other plants. They weren't mean like that scary tyrannosaurus. Plus," Keesha spread her arms and raised them to the sky, "they were as big as a house."

"I like the brontosaurus too," T-Bob said.

"Uh, it's been nice talking to you," the man said. "I guess we better be getting on. We've got a lot of ground to cover before the riverboat comes back to pick us up."

"It's been nice talking to you," T-Bob said and watched them walk past. He lifted his hand and waved. "Bye, Keesha."

As her mother pulled Keesha along, she turned her head and said, "Bye."

The smile on her face made T-Bob's heart melt. *It must be nice having a wife and kids*, he thought. He knew he was special and couldn't have kids.

His mother told him to pretend animals were his children. At home, he had three inside cats and two outside dogs. They were all strays, and he gave them a home. The pets couldn't have children either. So, they were all just one big happy family.

T-Bob looked at his watch and saw it was nearing time to give snacks to the big cats. As he marched down the sidewalk, a warm wind blasted unexpectedly and rattled the trees. Leaves shook free of the branches and paratrooped around him.

T-Bob looked up to the sky. Something didn't feel right. He couldn't put his finger on it, but something was wrong.

Then, T-Bob heard the territorial, foghorn-like growl coming from the albino alligator exhibit. Something had disturbed it too.

A hippopotamus expressed its anxiety with its laugh-like bellow, prompting a lion to unleash a vicious roar, and an elephant to sound its trumpet-like warning.

T-Bob picked up his pace. Cold chills walked up his spine, just like the time a bear broke free of its cage, and no one knew where it was for half a day.

*

Broderick Brown stretched his elbows behind his back and yawned. Today was his first day off from work in over three weeks. Pulling twelve-hour shifts at the Shell refinery offered Dionne, his wife, and daughter, Keesha, a comfortable life. Working those long periods without a day off also took a toll on his body. He so wanted to sleep in before spending the day with his family. But, his body had adjusted to waking up at 4 a.m. every morning, and today was no exception. He eventually got out of bed at 6 a.m., becoming tired of staring at the ceiling.

"What time did you go to sleep last night?" Dionne asked while keeping an eye on Keesha as she ran around underneath a sixty-foot replica of a brontosaurus.

Breaking from his reverie, Broderick said, "Huh? Uh, I fell asleep on my couch around eight."

"Shift work isn't only destroying our marriage, its also shortening your life," Dionne said.

"Well, I certainly would sleep better in my own bed and not that sleeper-sofa in the apartment."

Dionne turned her gaze to him, and said, "Don't try to guilt your way into coming back home. The only time we got to see you was when you worked days. But then you came in, showered, ate, and then fell asleep on your easy-chair. You hardly spoke a word to us, and when you did, you were just a big grump."

"I've got to work to pay the bills. I don't have a college education, and no one else will pay as much as the refinery,"

Broderick said, realizing his caustic tone would not add any points to his defense.

"But *do* you have to work nearly every day of your life?"

"You just don't understand. We're short-handed right now. There's a turnaround on another unit, and some of the guys went over there. We've got to man *our* unit. Plus, if I want to get into management, I need to be there whenever they need me."

"You've been telling me *they're short-handed* for the last ten years." Dionne's ire suddenly melted. She closed her eyes and held back tears. Composing herself, she said, "I don't want to fight anymore. I…isn't there some way you can get a straight day job? A job where you can be home every afternoon with Keesha and me? A job where you can spend time with your friends and family on weekends? I'm tired of living my life like a single parent."

Broderick rubbed his brow. He felt Dionne's anguish and could only imagine Keesha's disappointment in him not being a stronger presence in her life. But what was he to do? Many times he *was* forced to work, just because no one else was available. Though he was honest enough to admit, he hated to pass up on any overtime. It was like leaving money on the table, and his sense of greed wouldn't allow him to do that. But that way of thinking had gotten him where he was today—living alone in some cheap apartment. Why was he working so hard to be so miserable?

"Dionne, I don't know if I can do enough to fix things between us. There's only so much control I have at work over my schedule. But I can tell you this," now *he* fought to hold back tears, "when I get back to work on Monday, I'll see if I can get on a shift that might keep me from working more of my off days."

"You will? Seriously?" she asked.

The disbelief in her voice hurt Broderick to the core. This might be the last chance he had at saving his marriage. He hoped to goodness he could deliver on his commitment. "I promise." He meant what he said, but he knew deep down that passing on overtime would challenge him like an alcoholic passing on free booze.

"Daddy," Keesha called. "Come see this funny looking lizard." Then, she gasped.

Broderick turned his gaze over to his daughter. She had moved away from the brontosaurus and over to some low hedges.

He felt so weak, he wanted to fall on his knees and beg forgiveness for failing his family.

But Dionne had turned one eye to him. Her gaze let him know she timed how fast he responded to his daughter's request.

"I'm coming, baby," Broderick said, straightening his shoulders, and going to the beck and call of his daughter's needs under the watchful eye of his assessor.

As he approached, something rustled through the hedges. "What was it?"

Keesha bit her lip and bobbed her head as she tried to see past foliage. "Shoot, it ran away."

"Was it one of those green lizards the cat likes to leave at the doormat?" Broderick asked.

"No, Daddy. Those lizards have four legs and are flat on the ground. At first, I thought it was a lizard that stood on two legs and had short arms. Then, I saw its tail when it ran off. It was a baby dinosaur."

"You're pulling my leg, right?" Broderick then laughed.

"No, Daddy. I'm serious. It looked like a baby *compsognathus*."

"A *what*?

"Compsognathus. *Comp-sog-na-thus*," Keesha said.

Broderick looked over at Dionne's accusing gaze. Had his relationship with his daughter suffered so badly that she resorted to making up stories to vie for his attention? Turning back to Keesha, he said, "Baby, dinosaurs don't exist anymore. You know that."

"But I *saw* it!" Keesha said.

"You've got dinosaurs on the brain. You just made a mistake. Maybe somebody's pet iguana got loose, and that's what you saw."

Keesha's eyes widened, and her jaw dropped. "Daddy," her voice shook, "there's a *troodon* coming up behind you."

Okay, now things were going too far. "Keesha, you and I need to have a little talk. Making up stories—"

"Broderick!" Dionne screamed.

He turned and saw the interloper. At first, his mind worked double-speed trying to make sense of it. They were at a dinosaur exhibit at the zoo, and he had seen more than enough stationary recreations, along with a few with animated features. As much as he wanted to make the dinosaur before him a man-made robot, the fluid motion of the creature and the sharp teeth lining its open mouth forced him to accept the impossible.

His heart skipped a few beats as he raised his hands toward the troodon and yelled out a warning.

Dionne darted behind him and hugged tightly onto Keesha.

The troodon moved with uncertainty forward. Its reptilian head slowly snaked from side to side, and its beady yellow eyes fixated on the humans before it. The claws on its three-fingered hands looked deadly but didn't compare to the claws on its feet.

There weren't as many people at the zoo today as Broderick had expected, which now proved to be a blessing. Knowing the consequences of his next move, he looked quickly about to make sure there weren't any innocent bystanders in the background.

The troodon's bravery increased to the point of attack. It hissed in defiance and sped toward its prey.

Reaching underneath his shirt, Broderick pulled a pistol from the pancake holster in the small of his back. He brought the .45 caliber up, flicking the switch on the laser. The green light raced about the troodon's chest until he steadied his aim with his left hand.

Near point-blank range, he squeezed the trigger twice in rapid succession.

The troodon yelped, Dionne and Keesha screamed, and Broderick took the brunt force of the charging dinosaur.

He hadn't been plowed like that since being blindsided on a kickoff return in high school. His head went back, and he saw blue sky before his head bounced on the ground. The gun flew out of his hands, and the breath left his lungs.

Fire blazed through his ribs as claws breached flesh. His hands free, he grabbed hold of the troodon's neck and dug in his thumbs trying to crush its windpipe.

Dionne, crying for help, raced a few steps over and picked up the pistol. Pointing the gun, she warned, "Get off him! Get off him!"

Despite the pain and panic, Broderick realized the troodon had stopped moving. Its mouth was closed, and the claws weren't digging into his chest.

Struggling to get on his side, he finally found leverage and pushed the dead dinosaur off with his hands and knees.

"Broderick, are you okay?" Dionne asked as Keesha wailed in the background.

"I don't know," he said, jumping up and away from the dead troodon. He snatched the gun from her hand and laid aim again on the prehistoric creature.

"Oh, Broderick, you're bleeding. Oh my God!" Dionne said and broke into tears.

He stepped over to the troodon and cautiously kicked it in the belly. No sign of any life.

Backing away with the laser painting the troodon's head, he finally put the gun away when he reached his wife's side.

"Does it hurt?" Dionne asked.

Keesha ran and wrapped her arms around his waist.

His left hand patted her shoulder, and his right hand gingerly touched the left side of his chest. His cotton shirt was cut and wet with blood. Near as he could tell, the claws didn't go much beyond skin deep.

The dinosaur had died as soon as it was shot. Lucky for him, he had a large caliber handgun and a laser to aid his aim; even luckier that he maintained his composure enough to hit the target at all.

"I'm okay," he said. He looked around and suddenly felt exposed. There was no one else in sight. The gunshots were sure to drive everyone away. It would only be a matter of time before the authorities arrived to investigate. He wondered if he should remove the gun from his possession and place it on the walk for all to see. With his family there, he didn't want to be armed and take the chance that a nervous officer would misjudge the situation and do something horrific.

"Hey! Hey, Keesha's parents!" a familiar voice called out from behind a palm tree on a corner.

Broderick couldn't see the man, only the square ended shovel he held, but knew it was T-Bob from earlier. "It's okay, T-Bob. You can come over." He hoped T-Bob could make some sense of all of this but seriously doubted it.

Carrying the shovel with both hands, the handle at a 45° angle across his chest, T-Bob marched to the scene ready for battle. "I heard gunshots. Did y'all hear gunshots?"

"Yeah, we heard them," Broderick said, wondering how T-Bob would take the news if he told the employee he had done the shooting.

"What happened to that dinosaur exhibit?" T-Bob asked as he stepped up to the dead creature.

"T-Bob, that's not a model. That's a real dinosaur," Broderick said.

T-Bob's eyes lost focus. His pursed lips rose and almost touched his nose. "There aren't supposed to be real dinosaurs here."

As simple-minded as T-Bob seemed, he reasoned the circumstances well. "I agree. And believe me, I wish this one wasn't here now," Broderick said.

Screams rose in the distance; coming from near the entrance to the zoo. Something in the tone of those cries reached out and latched icy-cold fingers around Broderick's inner core. Sheer horror electrified the air, building an invisible cage.

Broderick needed to get his wife and daughter to safety but didn't know which way to turn.

More death-screams erupted from different parts of the zoo. Various animals joined in protest to whatever threatened their sedentary lifestyle.

"Daddy, more dinosaurs are coming," Keesha said and pointed.

Broderick whipped his head over and saw a creature as tall as a Great Dane lurking near a patch of bamboo. This bipedal dinosaur had bird and reptile characteristics. The short arms had feathers but were far from wings capable of flight. An olive-green swath ran from the top of its skull all the way down its tan, spotted body to a tail that made the dinosaur near ten feet long.

The deinonychus had yet to spot the humans. Broderick wanted to keep it that way as he realized bullets might not be enough to protect them this time.

"There's another one, Daddy," Keesha said.

Broderick felt his daughter tightening her grip around his waist. "T-Bob, is there a place we can hide?"

"Yeah," T-Bob said as if a thought had surprised him. "The reptile house. It was built to withstand a hurricane. We rode out Katrina in there. I have keys to all the exhibits here."

Never taking his gaze off the two raptor-like dinosaurs, Broderick said, "T-Bob, move at a slow, steady pace until we get out of sight of those creatures.

"Dionne, you follow T-Bob and take Keesha by the hand. I'll follow and keep an eye on them."

T-Bob closed an eye and nodded. He pushed his jaw forward and led the way.

CHAPTER 8

The MSY control tower exploded with cheers when Co-pilot Jim Hall radioed in that Captain Wesselman had successfully landed the 737 on the Mississippi River.

Ritchie Lamoine knew it wasn't time to declare victory. It was up to the Coast Guard and any other support vessels in the area to rescue the passengers and bring them safely ashore. Still, the historic landing of a 737 on the Mississippi River without the plane flying apart was destined to be named the *Miracle on the Mississippi*.

"Hey, Ritchie. Come over here," Mark Chaney called out. The air traffic controller hunched over his control station with his gaze glued to the radar screen.

"Are those things *still* there?" Ritchie asked.

"Yeah, but they aren't as bunched up as before. They're circling overhead, posing a threat to the whole airport," Mark said.

This is why they pay me the big bucks, Ritchie thought. Shutting down MSY would severely impact flight travel in the whole US and jilt some international flights over the rest of the globe. He had the authority to make that decision, which would cost airlines millions and millions of dollars.

There was no way he could close the airport without explaining the imminent threat. How would he do that and sight *danger from flying pterodactyls* as the reason? He'd be sent directly to the nut house. But, lives were in danger. Whatever heat came his way, he'd just have to endure until he had hard evidence to back him up.

Ritchie turned a switch on his radio to connect to every air traffic controller in the tower, and said, "Attention. Due to unknowns threatening the airspace, I am suspending all departures at this time. Contact all inbound and redirect to other airports."

Those words were simple enough to say. The burden he had just placed on controllers, airports, pilots, and passengers, though, was unimaginable. Controllers' scowls and blank faces of disbelief looked back at him.

"You have your orders," he said.

"Ritchie," Mark said. "Got an F-fifteen heading from the Gulf returning to Belle Chasse. Maybe you can contact them and see if that jet can fly over and scare those things away from the airport."

"I don't know if that's a good idea. The jet would be at risk too."

"The pterodactyls are at three thousand feet. If he flies above that, he'll be okay. We need to clear the airspace. Make those things move out of here," Mark said. "He can't fire his guns at them. But maybe a couple of flybys would work."

That wasn't a bad idea. A huge chunk of metal harassing the interlopers might send them scurrying.

Ritchie hurried over to his desk and looked at a laminated sheet scribed with important phone numbers. Finding the number for the Naval Air Station Joint Reserve Base located a short twenty miles south, he punched in the number on the phone.

Why hadn't the pterodactyls moved on already? They continued to circle above the airport as if drawn to it like a magnet. He didn't know how much of a threat they would pose to the public, but this was the worst possible place for those strange creatures to be.

If the F-15 could shoo the pterodactyls away, MSY might be back up in business in a few hours. That would certainly put a feather in his cap. Of course, he'd take all the credit for thinking outside of the box. That's how's he came to be *making the big bucks* anyway. Stepping on the backs of fellow workers had made him rise to the top.

The Naval Air Station operator answered.

Ritchie was on his way to a fat bonus at the end of the year.

*

Lieutenant Kevin 'Nuke' Tassin cruised at five hundred seventy m/hr over the depleting swamps and marshlands of Louisiana's coast, heading back to base. Protecting the Gulf's coast from foreign intruders for the last ten years had given him a personal perspective of the erosion few shared. This was a crisis happening in real time. In fact, it was said Louisiana lost a football field of landmass every hour. There were a few programs in place to help restore the wetlands. One program collected old Christmas Trees after the holidays and fortified the coastal muck with them. That made people feel better, but the action was as effective as blocking a river flow with a toothpick.

Kevin felt blessed, though. He grew up in the neighboring St. Bernard Parish, in the historic city of Chalmette. *Chalmations*, as they referred to themselves, were a tight community of unique individuals, bound by culture and local customs. They thought of themselves so highly, that if you asked one of them where they were from, they would simply say *the Parish*. Louisiana had Parishes, whereas in the rest of the US, the states were divided into *counties*.

The actual Battle of New Orleans took place in Chalmette. The Chalmette Battlefield memorial and cemetery were part of the Jean Lafitte National Historical Park and Preserve, and he had visited many times over the years.

Kevin made his move back near his hometown after an overseas tour in 2007. Hurricane Katrina in '05 had flooded St. Bernard Parish so severely that less than a half dozen homes out of twenty-seven thousand were habitable. He wanted to be closer to home to help his friends and family rebuild.

"Nuke, how's your fuel?" the Belle Chasse air traffic controller said over his headphones.

"Fuel's good, *Catahoula*," Kevin said. "It will be a while before I yell *bingo*."

"More importantly, how's your bladder?"

"Not so bad that I can taste the piss yet. I can always hang my *lizard* out the window if I need to. What's up? I'm down to ten *angels* and coming in to land," Kevin said, thinking he was too close to base to be sent back to the Gulf on another mission.

"Got a report on a number of *bogeys* circling MSY."

"*Bogeys*? UFOs?"

"MSY described them as *large unidentified birds*."

"Let me get this straight in my head. You want me to go to MSY and check out a flock of birds? Really? My cannons don't shoot corn."

"Believe it or not, it's enough of a problem to close the whole airport to all air traffic. MSY requested you to make a flyby and hopefully drive them away."

"Roger, Catahoula. Scare tweety-birds away from MSY International," Kevin said with obvious sarcasm. He had a twinge of excitement when he thought he might get a chance to chase another UFO. He had only one encounter with what would qualify as a genuine unexplained aircraft event.

A few years ago, he responded to a call in Plaquemines Parish. He had the bogey on his radar for over a full minute before it disappeared. The investigators concluded the UFO was nothing more than swamp gas. How anyone thought he could track swamp gas on radar was beyond him.

"The bogeys' ceiling is three *angels*. You'll be going in *blind*, so don't get cocky and get too low. Engine turbines don't chew fowl very well."

"Roger, Catahoula. I don't need a wingman for this mission," Kevin said while adjusting his computer for MSY International. "Going *buster* for MSY. Will drop it to four *angels* on approach. You better get the fire trucks ready, and the hoses charged up."

"Why? You expecting a crash and burn?"

"No, I'm going to scare those birds so badly, it going to rain white and paint the runway like it's fresh snow."

"Roger, Nuke," Catahoula said and chuckled. "Switch from UHF to VHF civilian communication band. When you're done, radio back and *RTB*."

"Roger, Catahoula," Kevin said. "Make sure to ice down the Abita beer for the crawfish boil tonight. I'm ready to *suck heads* and *pinch tails*."

"Roger, Nuke. I'll hand you a cold one when you step off the jet. Over."

"Roger. Over," Kevin said. There was no need to hit his afterburners to go *buster* to get to MSY. He was just acting *over-the-top* with control. The airport was less than thirty miles away. He'd have to throttle back now to make a safe approach at two hundred m/hr.

*

Kevin had visited little of the city of New Orleans in the last few years. Things just weren't the same as he remembered. Lots of restaurants, bars, and retail establishments had closed because of hurricane Katrina or simply became a victim of changing times. Benny's Blues Bar, Uglesich's restaurant, McKenzie's Bakery, even K&B Drugs. *Ain't dere no more*, Kevin thought in local slang.

Hubigs Pies had burned to the ground in 2012. Man, he sure missed those hand-sized fried pies! Chocolate and peach were his two favorites.

It was time for him to check in. *"Where you at*, MSY? This is Lieutenant Kevin 'Nuke' Tassin. Coming to you live via JASJRBNO. Over," Kevin said as the Mississippi River passed underneath.

"Roger, Nuke," the controller said. "The unknowns are still in the area at three thousand feet. Approach with caution."

"Roger. Too bad I don't have birdshot in my guns. Y'all would cook up a bird gumbo if I did."

"Sounds tasty, Nuke. I know you Cajun's will eat anything, but I believe I'd have to pass anyway," the controller said.

"You must be one of them *Yankees*," Nuke said, knowing the controller's Southern twang marked him as a native.

"Not me. I just grew up on the other side of the swamp. I speak fluent *Red Neck*, though. You know, Bud Lite, Coors Lite, and Miller Lite," the controller said. "Let me know when you have a visual."

"Come in, Nuke," a different voice said from MSY.

"Go ahead."

"I went to high school with a *Kevin Tassin*. This is *Ritchie Lemoine*."

"Yeah, Ritchie. We worked at that machine shop our senior year. Glad to see you made something of your life other than being a grease monkey."

"You too. Must be a hoot flying a jet for the military. After this is over, we need to get together and have a beer. I'm buying."

"You're on. Coming up to the airport now," Kevin said. A few miles to the east, a flare from the Shell refinery licked up toward the heavens. The roaring flame made him wonder how many sacks of crawfish a burner that size would boil.

Kevin expected to see a large black cloud hovering over the airport. Instead, he saw what looked like small aircraft circling. But these creatures were certainly not aircraft. They weren't birds either.

"I've got a visual, MSY. But I'm not sure I know how to report," Kevin said. "Kinda reminds me of flying dinosaurs I watched on *Land of the Lost* when I was a kid."

"We understand, Nuke. From down here they look like pterodactyls. But we were reluctant to put that in our call to Belle Chasse."

"Roger, MSY. I'd be in my easy-chair back at the base nibbling off a six-pack if you had. I can't take any photos, but I can get a radar shot of this for the boys back at the base to look at later."

He flipped the switch on his *look down/shoot down radar* and banked to get an above advantage over his targets. *Who dat say who dat when I say who dat?* Kevin thought to himself as he often did when befuddled.

Cheating a little, he dropped below three and a half angels before locking in his radar. The radar distinguished low flying objects from ground clutter. The cross-section footprint of these bogeys was unlike anything he had seen before.

After a few seconds of observation, most of the bogeys began a rapid descent toward the tower. Falling almost as if he *had* shot them out of the sky. A few, however, did the opposite and climbed upward.

When Kevin's imminent collision alarm lit up the cockpit, he realized he had pushed fate too much by dropping too low. He immediately thrust the throttle forward and pulled back on the tiller, trying to gain altitude as quickly as possible. Unfortunately, a quick escape wasn't in the cards.

The creature flew by too fast for him to get much of a look. When it hit his left wing, his teeth nearly rattled out of his head.

Multiple alarms made the cockpit sound like an old video arcade. The left engine flamed out. Half of the left wing was missing. The vertical stabilizer was damaged and the left horizontal stabilizer inoperable.

The jet banked hard port side. Kevin gripped the tiller so tightly that he thought he'd never be able to open his fingers again. The jet did everything in its power to stabilize, but it was a losing battle.

I'm in deep doo-doo, Kevin thought. He would have to put the forty-five thousand pound bird down and eject. With no time to spare, the only vacant area nearby was right underneath him. The airport runway was clear, and he didn't have to worry about the fireball starting any inadvertent fires.

Already so low to the ground, he pointed the jet's nose downward and pulled the ejection seat firing handle. Explosive cartridges blew the canopy off and detached the seat. Then, powerful rockets blasted underneath lifting him upward.

The shock his body felt was ten times worse than the earlier collision. With all the dangers pilots faced during flight, the whole time they were strapped to explosives. That thought struck Kevin as ironic as the rockets lifted him higher, and he briefly wondered if the system meant to save him might malfunction and be the death of him.

Then, the parachute deployed. Kevin had his world inverted as the chute caught air and snagged him back toward the Earth. His body left the tight embrace of the seat's straps, and faster than he would have liked, the runway sped toward him.

Kevin heard his F-15 smash to the concrete a few hundred feet away. The ensuing fireball towered into the air as he caught a glimpse before his boots hit terra firma.

Dropping and rolling, as he'd trained to do, absorbed some of the impact from his fall. This was the first time he had ever landed on concrete, though. Hard earth was bad enough, but concrete was completely unforgiving.

Kevin flatted to his back as the parachute draped over him. He took a few seconds to push his mind past the adrenaline rush to do a self-health assessment. As near as he could tell, no bones had broken. His left foot and shoulder received the most abuse. All in all, he was in pretty good shape considering what he had just gone through.

As he dug his way out of the silky cloth that carried him safely to the ground, an occasional *pop* and *hiss* indicated his jet continued to burn. *Such a waste*, he thought. The F-15 cost more than he could make in fifty lifetimes. He removed his helmet and let it fall to the runway.

He emerged as shattering glass and dull thumps reverberated behind him. Turning, Kevin had a clear view of the creatures menacing the airport. And, yes, they were in fact, pterodactyls; which absolutely made no sense at all.

There must have been thirty or forty of them haphazardly flying about. Some had crashed into the control tower. Some had planted onto the runway, and others had smashed into terminal windows. The pterodactyls acted as if they were disoriented.

Then Kevin wondered what had attracted the creatures to the airport in the first place and remembered how they reacted when he turned on his look down/shoot down radar above them. *Radar*, he thought. That might be the connection. The tower's radar had attracted them, and his radar somehow upset the applecart. When the pterodactyls flew lower, the tower radar must have disrupted their sense of flight.

The scene was scarier than the flying monkeys on the Wizard of Oz, which, terrorized him as a child and still gave him goosebumps when he thought about them at night.

SKEER-AK!

Kevin shot his gaze toward the piercing cry. At first, the mass heading for him looked like a low flying jet. As his eyes focused, he realized it was another prehistoric creature, similar to a pterodactyl, but much larger.

Who dat say who dat when I say who dat? Kevin felt the icy grip of fear take hold of his spine.

The quetzalcoatlus landed ungracefully ten yards away.

As it uprighted itself, Kevin thought it was the strangest looking creature he had ever seen in real life or even in the movies. It was at least twenty feet tall. Its front arms served as front legs, and the pointed wing tips folded neatly away from the ground. The neck stretched from its body to its skull by over ten feet. Brownish hair covered the neck and body. Its stork-like beak didn't appear to have any teeth when it opened its mouth to let out another shriek. The beautiful green crown on its head looked out of place—like it had been painted on.

The only animal the creature reminded him of was a giraffe. Both had the same long necks. If a giraffe had a beak and wings, it would look similar to what stood before him now.

The quetzalcoatlus' bobbing head stabilized, and the creature's beady eyes locked onto him.

I'm in deeper doo-doo now.

SKEER-AK!

Kevin reached into his survival vest and pulled out his Sig Sauer M11. A pilot carrying a sidearm while not flying over enemy territory had always seemed stupid. The pistol grip had a way of digging into his ribs during flight. Now, he was glad to have endured that discomfort.

The quetzalcoatlus tested its claws on the concrete and eased toward Kevin.

He squeezed off two rounds toward its torso, and the creature did not indicate that it'd been hit. The hulking mass of overgrown turkey might not feel much from a 9mm bullet. Kevin would have better luck at stopping it if he could shoot it in the eye. There was little to no chance of doing that.

It was time to leave.

Looking for an escape path, he saw a fuel truck in front of the fuel depot next to the freight terminal. That and the dying fire from his F-15 gave him an idea.

He fired two more rounds and dashed over to the ejection seat not far away and found the attached emergency kit. Unsecuring the kit, Kevin shot two more times and made a bee-line for the fuel truck.

SKEER-AK!

At this point, he wasn't sure if the bullets harmed the creature or just annoyed it. Didn't matter as long as he —

CRACK! The quetzalcoatlus had extended its neck and snapped its six-foot beak right at the edge of Kevin's backside. The beak made contact and tore off a piece of his flight jacket.

This was no time to turn and fight. His feet found extra speed, and the pain in his left foot went numb. There was no way of knowing how fast the creature could run, and Kevin kept waiting for that beak to chomp down and cut him in half.

SKEER-AK!

The pterosaur's shriek lifted Kevin's butt like the rockets underneath his ejection seat. The fuel truck loomed a short distance away. He was so close now—so close!

Pointing the pistol behind his head, Kevin fired three random shots—trying to give the creature pause now that it was this close.

Still amazed he hadn't been eaten, Kevin finally made it to the truck and put the white behemoth between him and the prehistoric creature.

SKEER-AK! The quetzalcoatlus' shadow cast over in front of Kevin as he hid by the driver's side of the truck. He holstered his pistol and unhooked the fuel nozzle, locking the handle.

With emergency kit in hand, he stepped over and hopped up into the cab.

To his relief, the ignition key was in place. He started the engine, with a huff of black smoke coming out of the front exhaust.

The diesel's roar held the creature at bay for the moment. But Kevin knew that wouldn't last long and had to go all in on his plan. He pulled a lever on the dash, and the PTO engaged the fuel pump.

From the side mirror, he saw a growing pool of aviation fuel as the nozzle gushed. He essentially rolled the dice that he could escape before static electricity or something else ignited the fuel.

Opening his door, he held onto the roof as he stood on his seat. He waved his free hand at the pterosaur, and yelled, "Hey! Hey! Hey!"

Kevin slinked back in as the quetzalcoatlus' ire pushed it past uncertainty. He rolled down the window and flailed both arms about. "Over here, *big bird*. Over here!"

The quetzalcoatlus took the bait and sauntered over near the driver's side.

Kevin climbed over the console onto the passenger's seat. Just as soon as he opened the door and dropped onto the pavement, the pterosaur's beak jabbed through the open window, reaching across to the passenger's side. Had he still been in the cab, he would have been shish kabob.

Petroleum light components stung his eyes and irritated his nose as his boots splashed onto the concrete. He had to get far enough away before lighting this candle, or he'd be committing suicide. But, he had to hurry. The creature would leave the area and come after him once he caught its eye.

SKEER-AK!

Too late. It had spotted him. Kevin opened the emergency kit as he ran and pulled out the flare gun. He wasn't even a hundred feet away when he aimed and fired.

The flare *popped* as it jettisoned forward, streaking like a Roman candle, and landing in the growing lake of fuel.

Fire spread as fast as lightning, engulfing the fuel truck and the quetzalcoatlus in raging flames.

SKEER-AK! The creature's cry was different this time; its rage replaced with pain. It spread its massive wings as it readied to fly.

Kevin watched in awe at the incredible sight. The wingspread must have been over thirty feet! But this was no time to watch the firebird. The fuel truck's safety valve screeched to the sky as heat overpressured the tank.

Kevin took out running again and headed toward one of the terminals. His left foot really started to hurt now, but he dared not slow and take any chances.

When the fuel truck exploded, it dropped Kevin to his knees. He rolled on the ground, bumping his head on concrete, and came to rest on his back. A fireball rose into the sky as high as the moon before consciousness faded to black.

He woke not long later and felt a knot on the back of his head. It was sore to the touch, but his head felt clear. Good thing he hadn't been any closer to the explosion.

The small burning heap next to the truck indicated the pterosaur's fate.

Good.

Kevin rose and headed to the nearest terminal door when a window above crashed, and a woman and what resembled a dog fell to the pavement. The woman's head burst like a melon on impact.

As he neared, it became obvious that the animal was no dog. The creature looked like a combination of a bird and a reptile. It had a light blue colored head and looked lizard-like on a short neck. A brown feathered crest on its crown matched the feathers on its body. It had small wings on short arms and deadly looking claws on its hands and feet.

There was no saving the woman. Kevin aimed his pistol as the velociraptor shook off the fall and stood. He fired the remainder of the fifteen round magazine until the slide sprang back and locked.

Pterodactyls and now this…*dinosaur*? Kevin looked around as if waiting for someone to pop up and clue him in on what was going on around there.

A human scream came from the concourse above. Whatever brought pterodactyls outside the tower had deposited invaders inside the airport too.

Kevin dropped his empty magazine and slapped in a full one. He pulled back the slide on his pistol and chambered a round.

It looked like the fun was just beginning.

*

"Everybody, get away from the windows!" Ritchie Lemoine yelled as he dropped his binoculars and dashed for safety.

A pterosaur hit the glass, shattering an 8x8 foot pane into a million pieces. The creature's body was larger than a man, and its triangular-shaped head and bat-like wings made it look twice as big.

Mark Chaney and the other three controllers spilled out of their chairs, rushing to the other side of the tower.

Dan Lewis made the unfortunate choice to take refuge by the window where the next prehistoric monster crashed through. The pterosaur's beak hit him dead center in his back and poked all the way through his chest.

The poor man's eyes bulged as he flailed his arms. His mouth formed silent words, and his face shook uncontrollably.

"Dan!" Mark yelled and darted over to his co-worker's side.

The first pterosaur was unconscious or dead.

But the one who had killed Dan was alive and well. It flapped its wings and shook its head, trying to free itself from the dead body. Its right claw struck Mark as he neared—sending the man backward and falling on his butt.

"Everyone, evacuate the tower!" Ritchie commanded.

The window behind him shattered, and the devious supervisor keeled over face-first as the third pterosaur smashed its way into the control tower.

The other two controllers followed orders and dashed to safety down the stairs.

Mark wasn't a hero, but four years in military service had taught him never to leave a fallen comrade.

Ritchie was at least alive; evident by his cries for help.

Mark's lip craved for a fresh dip, but that would have to wait.

Looking around, he searched for anything he might use as a weapon. Nothing caught his eye until he saw the cleaning supply storage closet.

He ran over and opened the door. The arsenal of weapons included chlorine bleach, an old-fashioned mop and bucket, two types of brooms, a dustpan, and a variety of glass cleaners.

Wishing he had his AK-47 or his M1 Garand, he had to improvise with what was available. The mop had a wooden handle, whereas the two brooms had thin metal handles.

Mark grabbed the mop by the head and at the other end of the handle, bringing it down over his thigh. The mop handle snapped in two, just as he planned, leaving a bruise on his leg that hopefully would have time to heal.

He now had a three-foot makeshift weapon. The splintered end sloped enough at an angle that it would do some damage penetrating flesh.

Pulling the dustpan from the door shelf, he bounded to Ritchie's aid.

The creature on top of Ritchie wasn't moving, but the other who had killed Dan flapped its wings and screeched.

For the moment, Ritchie was better off hiding underneath the pterosaur than getting within striking distance of the other creature.

It occurred to Mark, approaching the pterodactyl, with a stick and a dustpan for weapons, seemed incredibly stupid. The opened door leading to the stairwell beckoned him to run and save his behind now.

"Help!" Ritchie cried.

Dip, don't fail me now, Mark thought and swallowed a gulp of tobacco spit for a surge of nicotine to make him invulnerable.

The pterosaur spread its wings when he approached.

"Get! Get!" Mark yelled as he swiped the empty air between them with the broom handle. His best chance to win this situation was to get the over-sized lizard-bat to fly out the same way it had come in.

The pterodactyl attacked first, snaking its head forward, and biting at the stick.

Mark moved the stick to the side and slapped the beak with the dustpan. He didn't feel like one of the three hundred Spartans, but he knew this country boy had the grit in him to survive.

"Ritchie, I've got this thing busier than a cat trying to cover turds on a marble floor. Roll out from under that beast."

Clawed hands extended about a quarter of the way down the creature's wings. The right claw made a swoop for him, bringing the rest of the wing with it.

Mark jabbed the claw. The pterosaur squawked, but the wing caught his side and knocked him down.

"I'm almost out," Ritchie called.

The next thing Mark knew, a wide-open pointed beak headed straight for his face. He held the broom handle in both hands and stopped the deadly weapon's advance by shoving the stick between its maw.

The creature was strong. Mark's arm muscles screamed for relief. The head slowly edged ever so closer.

"I'm up," Ritchie called. "Looks like you're in a bind. I'll get help. You hang in there, buddy."

Mark wanted to hurl a few curses but couldn't spare the breath. His arms were just about to give out as the beady eyes of the monster neared.

Hank Williams Jr., Mark's spiritual guide, whispered in his ear. *A country boy can survive*!

Mark dug the dip out of his lip with his tongue and spat in the beaked lizard-bat's eyes.

It made a hellacious *caw* and pulled away, shaking its head, and flapping its wings.

But it loomed over him madder than a wet hen and ready to go in for the kill.

I'm coming home, Momma. Mark held the broom handle out in feeble defense.

A fourth pterodactyl crashed through the window and took down the threatening menace.

With no time to waste, Mark rolled off his back onto his feet. He bounded to the stairwell and began his descent.

Counting his blessings, he sang as he pounded down each step: *We're from North Dakota and South Louisiana. We can whip a pterodactyl's ass with a dustpan and broom handle. A country boy can survive. A country boy can survive!*

CHAPTER 9

Sam Miceli had his back against the safety rail on the top deck of the paddlewheeler Southern Queen. The bright red waterwheel pushing the boat up the Mississippi River splashed droplets of water on the back of his neck. New Orleans jazz, thick with the long reach of a throaty trombone, filtered up from the deck below.

A pleasant breeze cooled his forehead on the sunny day. His tongue felt a bit thick, though. Man, could he use a shot of gin right about now.

The wad of bills in his left front pocket pressed annoyingly against his thigh. Lady Luck had been kind to him earlier. He found the hot dice on the craps table in a private gaming room on deck one.

His last name, *Miceli*, was the only ticket he needed to get the invite to the illegal action. Being the grandson of the infamous Carlos Miceli, *The Godfather of the New Orleans Mafia*, had its privileges.

Three well-dressed goons stood not far away directly in front of him, with their backs against a wall that supported the observation deck. Each had their arms hanging down, with their hands folded neatly by their crotches.

The hoodlum in the middle wore a black fedora hat and chewed gum with the left side of his mouth open. He gazed snake-like with his head cocked to the side.

The other two looked like they could have been brothers. Both had dark sunglasses riding rosy, veinous noses on pockmarked faces. Their slicked back black hair shined with oil.

"You got something you want to tell us, pretty boy?" the middle goon asked.

"Excuse me, I don't think we've been introduced," Sam said.

"Not that it matters. My name's Percy Ray. The other two are *the boys*."

"Pleasure to meet all of you. But, no, gentlemen. I don't have anything *to tell you*, as you asked. I came outside to get a breath of fresh air," Sam said. "It's a nice day. Don't you love this? Steaming up the mighty Mississippi like they did a hundred and fifty years ago."

"Now that you have a belly full of *fresh air*, you coming back downstairs for some more action?" Percy Ray asked.

Sam dropped an eyebrow and closed one eye. "You know, I think I've had enough excitement for one day." He slowly nodded. "Besides, they're about to open the buffet, and I could go for some crab cakes right about now. You guys want to join me? My treat."

"Naw, we don't eat with double-crossers," Percy Ray said.

The goon on the left turned his head and spat on Sam's brown Salvatore Ferragamo shoes.

Sam looked at the wad of phlegm glistening in the sun and realized he would not charm his way out of this one. He rubbed the side of his face with an open hand, and said, "Uh, there must be some misunderstanding. You gentleman *do* know who I am, don't you?" It was three against one, and Sam knew even if it were one-on-one, he'd have little chance of walking away the victor. Playing the *family name card* seemed like the best offense.

Percy Ray shrugged. "You come from a very respected family. But that name don't carry the weight it used to. It's cheats like you who are responsible for that. You bring disrespect to your family name."

A young couple holding hands came around the corner. Both had bright smiles and the sparkle of love in their eyes.

Mr. Spits broke from Percy Ray's side and stood in front of them, with arms crossed over his chest.

The lovers' smiles melted, and they gazed blankly at each other.

Mr. Spits lowered his head and peered over his sunglasses at them.

The couple got the message and made a swift retreat.

"Time's wasting," Percy Ray said. "Hand over the cash you stole."

"Stole?" Sam said incredulously. "I won the money fair and square. It was my turn for Lady Luck to smile down on me."

"I don't think you understand," Percy Ray said. "My boss expects me to return the loot." He rubbed a knuckle under his chin. "Tell you what. You give us the money and the loaded dice, we'll let you go. If not…" he paused to chew gum, "we're gonna take the money and throw you in the paddlewheel."

The thought of getting mangled by the churning paddlewheel certainly got Sam's attention. But he was a *Miceli*. This threat could all be a bluff. Sure, he had scammed fifty thousand dollars from the craps game, but he desperately needed the money. There were other debts he had to make good outside of the Mafia. The Mexican drug cartel he owed was impatient and merciless.

Death by *Italian mobsters* or *Mexican monsters*. Sam felt a panic attack coming on. And when he panicked, he ran.

"Look! The police!" Sam shouted and pointed a finger to the left.

As the three goons took the bait and turned to look, he dashed to the right; hoping to make it past the wall supporting the observation deck and to the front promenade deck to mix in with the crowd.

Sam's luck rolled *snake-eyes* when the slick soles on his shoes couldn't adequately grip the moist deck. He spilled forward and landed flat on his stomach.

Percy Ray and company were on top of him before he could get up.

Looking even with Percy Ray's shoes, Sam lifted his gaze to the leader's eyes.

Bending over, Percy Ray scooped something off the deck. He lifted the dice up for his inspection and shook them about. "You should have done this the easy way."

The next thing Sam new, a size eleven loafer planted in his stomach, knocking his wind out.

"Get the money, and throw him over," Percy Ray ordered his goons.

Then, what seemed like a five-gallon bucket of water, rained down on Sam.

Percy Ray dropped the dice, and they bounced on the sopping deck.

Sensing danger, Sam lay flat on his back and saw a huge snake-ish head open its mouth and chomp down on Percy Ray's head. Long fang-like teeth in the front of the mouth pushed easily past human flesh and bone. Blood gushed down the leader's chest as he uselessly slapped the creature on the side of the head.

Briefly looking over the side, Sam saw the head attached to a neck over twenty feet long, connected to a massive gray body floating on the Mississippi's surface.

One goon pulled out a pistol and fired into the elasmosaur's neck.

The prehistoric creature felt the gun's onslaught and cried out in pain, slinging Percy Ray backward into the wall, where he crumpled into a bloody mess.

The elasmosaur clamped its jaws on the shooter's torso and jerked its head to the side, sending the gangster flying into the paddlewheel of the Southern Queen. His screams briefly breached over the patter of splashing water.

The last goon wanted no part of the sea monster. But as he turned and ran, he slipped on the deck too.

Once again, the snaking head claimed a prize. The elasmosaur sank its teeth in the goon's rear and hauled him over the railing and into the Mississippi.

Sam caught his breath for a second and gazed over at Percy Ray. The teeth had committed so much trauma to the mobster's head, there wasn't a chance he was still alive.

The gunshots would soon have others come to the back of the boat to investigate. Sam needed to leave and hide in the crowd before someone grabbed him for interrogation.

Picking up his loaded dice off the deck, he hurried toward the front of the boat. *Surely someone on the observation deck got a look at the creature*. There was no way anyone could pin Percy Ray's death on him, Sam hoped.

The promenade deck held a mass of people huddled together as far to the front as possible.

A young crewman grabbed Sam as he headed to blend in with the crowd.

"Sir, what happened back there? There were gunshots," the crewman said.

"Something big came out of the water. It looked like a dinosaur and had a neck so long that it was able to reach the top deck! Some guy had a gun and shot it when it attacked two of his buddies."

"Dinosaur? Mister, are you drunk? Do you have a gun?" the crewman asked.

"I'm not drunk, and I don't have a gun. You can search me. I just happened to be in the wrong place at the wrong time," Sam said.

"I saw it," one of the ship's sailors said from the observation deck. The man wore a blue uniform with gold bands around the sleeve, but Sam didn't think it was the captain. "I'm not sure what I saw. It was huge...reminded me of those dinosaurs in the ocean in that movie Jurassic World."

Sam's peripheral caught something reddish snaking up from behind the crowd. Its blade-like shape had the width of three men. Suction cups the size of beach balls dripped with the river's muddy funk. It looked just like the club at the end of a squid's tentacle. But the size of it was huge.

The tentacle crooked like a shepherd's hook and round, quivering suckers from its club mashed against two unfortunate passengers. The two men's screams had everyone fleeing from the front of the boat.

"What the...?" the crewman said as he spun toward the noise.

One of Sam's favorite appetizers was fried calamari. In fact, when he would fish off the Gulf with his uncle, he made him keep the cephalopods instead of using them for bait. Sam's mother made a marinara that turned average fried squid into a treat decadently delicious. Whatever was on the other end of the tentacle would be anything but.

Another tentacle came from below and searched the deck as the first tentacle disappeared with the two victims.

Sam knew squids had two feeding tentacles that were considerably longer than the eight other legs. He hoped those suction covered legs weren't trying to latch onto the boat's bottom. As scared as he was, he was so fascinated by the size of the squid, he couldn't pull his gaze away.

Then, bubbling of the port bow, the squid's stabilizing fin and mantle rose from the water, resembling a mountain shaped like the

Devil's horn. Its reddish skin glistened above the dark river. The beast looked otherworldly. Its majesty proclaimed that nothing on Earth could be its equal.

Its single eye peered out; a hungry black void wanting to suck out a man's will to live. The squid's body tilted backward revealing its parrot-like black beak. Sections of its eight arms, looking like massive rubber hoses, floated to the surface. The feeding tentacle snaked toward its open maw. The obsidian mechanism pushed through slimy white muscle and opened wide. The beak looked strong enough to snap an oak tree in half with a single bite.

The first man entered halfway in. The beak sliced the unfortunate victim in two above his waist. Face down, his arms slapped at the river's surface in a hopeless attempt to escape. Suffering was short-lived as the beak opened again. The rest of the man disappeared into the sea devil's mouth.

The second man flayed about uselessly. What horror he must have felt watching the first man meet such a dreadful fate!

The tentacle pulled toward the squid's mouth, and the beak took his upper body first. At least he was lucky enough to die a quick death.

Then, a young man dashed from mid-deck to the front, following along the railing. "Wow! Awesome!" His t-shirt proclaimed he was a fan of the University of Louisiana–Lafayette *Ragin' Cajuns*. "Eric! You gotta come see this!"

"Hey! Get away from there! Watch out!" Sam yelled, shocked at the display of stupidity.

In fascination, the young man apparently didn't notice the feeding tentacle sweeping the deck behind him.

The giant squid's pulsating bluish-white suction cups honed in on its prey.

Feeling powerless to help, Sam turned to run down the stairs to the next deck and spied a rectangular box on a wall. Big letters instructing to USE IN CASE OF EMERGENCY hung above a glass case guarding a fire ax.

His mind's eye saw what would happen next. The giant squid would claim its next prize and end another human life in a couple of bites. There was just something so wrong with that.

Sam ran up to the glass case and smashed it dead center with his right elbow. Shattered safety glass rained onto the deck, allowing him to grasp the ax handle and pull it free from its mount.

"AAAHHH!" the young man cried in the sea devil's grasp. The suction cups had planted on his back and his bare legs below his shorts.

Raising the ax above his head, Sam raced over to the tentacle just before it slinked over the side, and swung it downward with all his might.

The polished head of steel sliced deeply into quivering red flesh, sending a fountain of blood spewing into the air.

A shriek erupted from the river below never heard by human ears; sending an icy-bolt of fear up Sam's spine.

In a blink, the suction cup-laden club thrashed about, crashing the young man into Sam, and popping loose from the squid's hold.

Both men sprawled out on the deck as the injured feeding tentacle disappeared over the side.

"You okay?" Sam asked as he gathered his bearings and tried to roll to his knees.

"Yeah...I think so," the young man said.

"Jacob!" another young man called from by the stairwell, also wearing a *Ragin' Cajun* t-shirt. "What the heck happened to you?"

"Dude, you won't believe me when I tell you," Jacob said. He slowly stood and adjusted his shirt collar. Then he reached behind his left thigh. "Ow...that thing latched onto my leg so hard it broke the skin."

As Sam rose, using the ax handle as a crutch, he looked over the side and saw the squid's good feeding tentacle come straight for him.

With no time to react, the squid's wide club wrapped around him so tightly he couldn't breathe.

His feet left the deck, and as the tentacle pulled him over the side, his heart felt like it flew upward and hung in his throat.

The squid's mountainous red mantle jutted above the muddy river water. The ghastly one eye opened a gateway to Hell, and Sam felt like he was in the presence of Satan himself.

The black beak poked from the white membrane of its mouth.

This was it. Sam should have left when he could have and saved his own butt. He didn't know why he had felt a sense of obligation to risk his life for a stranger. As admittedly selfish as he was, that act of chivalry was beyond his normal character.

Maybe this had been his day to die all along. Rather than be taken out by the Mafia, God had given him one last chance to redeem himself before passing into the great beyond.

Sam felt the squid's grip loosen as the tentacle brought him nearer to the scissor-like beak. Then, as if toying with him, the suction cups let go of his legs and held tightly to his back—dangling him in the air above its open maw.

He still had the ax and swung it wildly about with one hand, doing his best to connect with flesh. His futile attempt didn't work, as the ax handle slipped from his sweaty grip and landed in the Mississippi.

Sam thought he heard the squid laugh as the black beak came closer. But no, he realized it wasn't laughter. It was a noise like people made when they anticipated something good to eat.

Sam's last contribution on Earth would be *um um good* to giant cephalopod.

Ironically, it was as if all the squids he had eaten in his life would get the ultimate revenge.

CHAPTER 10

Dr. Breaux's legs responded to the woman's cry for them to run before he realized what was going on. He heard pounding noises coming from inside Johnny Black's like something was trying to break through a wall.

Bridget was right next to him. He got the impression she could have sped past but instead maintained a half-step behind to keep him in her sight.

So far Bridget had remained strong through this ordeal. In fact, as the situation worsened, her fortitude increased.

Unlike him, he noticed. He was willing to hold off the troodon with that tiki torch at Pat O's to give Bridget enough time to escape. But she risked her life too to save his by dousing the dinosaur in vodka, which set it on fire. That was his last act of bravery—maybe his only moment of redemption after the entanglement experiment unleashed the prehistoric havoc. And now, now he seemed to vacillate between a coward too afraid to live or a coward whose only sense of preservation was to flee.

Bridget must certainly have realized this, and that's what kept him under her watchful eye.

Whatever tried to break into Johnny Black's had succeeded. It unleashed a terrifying warning that it chased after them.

"We've got to find shelter!" the woman cried out.

The young man leading the three strangers stopped and pulled on the door of the next business they came upon. The door was locked, and they continued to the next.

The door pulled open this time, tinkling a small brass bell hanging on the backside. The young man held the door open, and a short, portly man running with his arms extended while balancing a drink in his hands went through first.

Taking a moment to glance behind, he saw Bridget narrow her eyes and nod, a command for him to stay in line and not waver from his path.

Breaux also saw a feathered dinosaur that certainly was as tall as Big Bird from Sesame Street but looked like Satan himself had remade it in his own image. The theropod opened its mouth and hiss-roared again making Breaux feel like his bowels were about to unleash as he ran.

The young man called for them to hurry as he continued to man the door.

Sliding to a near stop, he bumped the door with his shoulder and entered, spilling inside the business.

Bridget followed, and the young man hurried in and closed the door, twisting the thumbturn on the deadbolt lock.

Everyone in the room dove to the floor, trying to find a hiding spot from view of the window.

The Utahraptor stopped by the front of the business.

Breaux peeked from the side of a display counter he hid behind and watched the dinosaur bend over and sniff the sidewalk. When it raised its head, it cried out in surprise and opened its mouth. At first, he thought the dinosaur had spotted one of them, but then realized it must have seen its reflection from the glass. That was a good thing, as he hoped the mirror-like glass would prevent the beast from seeing inside.

Not finding food or threat, the Utahraptor turned its attention elsewhere and lumbered out of sight.

The tension in Breaux's back released, and he put his butt on the floor and rested his back on the display counter. "It's gone," he whispered to Bridget, who had laid flat on the floor behind the same counter.

Then, the professor heard what sounded like a straw sucking the last remnants of liquid mixed with air from a cup.

The portly man poked his head from around an antique wardrobe. He let the straw drop from his lips, and said, "I think it's gone."

The young man and the woman appeared from their hiding places and went over to the other man.

Bridget rose to her feet and glanced their way, and then turned her gaze to him. "Doc, are you okay?"

Yeah, he was fine, but if that business' door had been locked, it might have been a different story for all of them. "Yes."

"Everyone else okay?" she said, having turned her attention to the strangers.

"We're fine," the woman said while giving the portly man the evil eye.

"I'm Bridget Reed, and this is Dr. Bryan Breaux. We're over here from Tulane. Doc is a professor there, and I'm a student."

"I'm Kathy Stevens. I'm with Delta airlines, as you might be able to tell from my flight attendant uniform."

"Dave Einstein. I'm a student at Tulane, too."

"I thought you looked familiar. I've probably seen you around the student union," Bridget said. "Although all you flannel wearing, bearded white dudes tend to look alike sometimes."

All gazes turned to the portly man, who smiled widely at the sudden attention. "Me...I'm *drunk*!" He laughed like an eight-year-old getting his feet tickled.

Kathy's face turned red, and she balled up her right hand into a fist.

"Okay...okay. My name is Melvin Posey. I own several used car dealerships in Cleveland."

"Any idea what's going on around here? One minute we're having drinks, and the next minute a triceratops and a T. rex are fighting it out in the street," Kathy said.

Bridget turned a warning gaze to Breaux that told him to be careful what he said.

"We were across the street at Pat O'leary's when the dinosaurs attacked. They seemed to appear collectively in the two bars leading to the patio. Bridget and I were celebrating my new..." Breaux caught himself before he created a trail to a place he didn't want to go, "new *promotion*. When they invaded the patio, we escaped by climbing onto the roof. When you three ran out of Johnny Black's, we had just come down from there."

"I just realized I haven't looked at my cell phone yet since the dinosaurs appeared," Dave said. He unclipped the phone from the holder and typed in his passcode. "Hmm, no bars."

The others, except for Melvin, pulled out their phones and checked.

"Mine was in my carry-on," Melvin said to no one in particular.

The negatives were unanimous.

"Dinosaurs are running in the streets of the French Quarter. I don't see any viable solution until the military moves in and destroys every last one of them. We'll just have to wait it out here," Breaux said.

"I wonder if there's any food or drink in this store? We'll need something if we're going to be here a while," Bridget said as she looked about.

"I've got some cherries in my drink," Melvin said as he looked over at Kathy. "I'll share them with everyone." It was an obvious attempt to quench Kathy's ire.

Dave pointed to the window, and said, "We're in Cou-Yon's Collectibles. These junk shops don't usually carry refreshments."

Breaux let his gaze wander about the room and saw nothing of the sort. There was jewelry, coins, furniture, figurines, and other knick-knacks, but nothing for sustenance.

"Oowee. Look at all the old coins over there," Melvin said.

"Hold it right there, Stinky," Kathy said grabbing onto his arm as he started for a display counter. "This stuff isn't yours for the taking. We're here to hide out, and that's all. You could get us in trouble."

Breaux didn't know why Kathy had called Melvin, *Stinky*, but considering the way the man looked and what he did for a living, it didn't take too much imagination to guess a plausible answer.

Stinky's head bobbled as he turned his gaze to meet Kathy's. The left corner of his mouth rose, and then the right corner of his mouth dropped. "I...don't...feel...so...good." His knees gave way, and he dropped to the floor.

"Gosh, darn it!" Kathy said through gritted teeth. "I told you not to drink all of that alcohol."

The portly man was on his side and rolled over on his back. Blinking his eyes like he was trying to get them to focus, he said, "No...that's not it." He closed his eyes and swallowed. "I need my...insulin. I'm a diabetic."

"I can give you your shot," Bridget said. "Is your pin in your jacket pocket?"

His eyes half-open, he shook his head. "In my carry-on with my phone."

Kathy looked up at the others. "Well, this is just great."

"Forgot to shoot-up…this morning. Need insulin…might die—" Stinky's eyes closed. His head cocked to the side, and his mouth dropped open wide.

Taking a deep breath, Kathy said, "Was he being dramatic? That drink he had was nearly pure alcohol."

"No, it looks like he's drifted into a diabetic coma," Bridget said.

"How bad is that? Does he just need to sleep it off?" Kathy asked.

"No, it's really bad," Bridget said. "It could lead to brain damage or death. We have to get that man his insulin."

"There's a pharmacy three blocks up St. Peter," Dave said.

"But the dinosaurs…" Breaux said and suddenly felt petty for his disregard of the used car king's health.

"Three blocks is not that far," Bridget said. "We can't sit here and let him die. That would make us responsible for his death."

Leave it to Bridget to put things in honest perspective. She essentially built a wall with only one door leading out. Did anyone have the nerve to selfishly choose to stay and not risk their life for another? Breaux knew *he* wanted that, but this whole mess was his fault to begin with.

"He's a big man," Dave said. "It will be difficult to carry him."

"Yeah, but he's short, and fat doesn't weigh as much as muscle," Kathy said. "Let's look around this place. Maybe we can find a table with wheels…or something we can use to make a stretcher."

Breaux watched as the other three split and searched the store. Even though his heart wasn't into it, he went through the motions and did the same.

He meandered over to a display case holding antique firearms. They were of the flintlock variety and useless as a weapon. Two items in the case caught his eye.

Laying on a red velvet cloth, a polished Confederate Cavalry Officer's Saber gleamed under the fluorescent lighting. The price tag showed the happy customer could take it home for the meager price of $6,750; which was a lot more than the cash he had in his pocket or even the limit on his credit card.

"Hey, I think I found something we can use," Dave said.

Breaux heard cyclical squeaking and turned and saw the young man pushing an old wheelbarrow. It had a rusty looking bed and a solid rubber tire. The handles looked in decent shape.

So, it appeared they would leave soon. If they were going to make a run for it, it only made sense to arm themselves.

Breaux and his roommate were part of the fencing team in college. He was among the best, if he did say so himself. That seemed forever ago, though.

He walked behind the counter and opened the display from the rear. He picked up the sword and held it in front of him. The sword was heavier than his fencing saber, but the balance felt nice. Using it in an actual battle would slow down some of his moves.

Next to the officer's sword, a Confederate D-Guard Bowie knife waited for purchase for $7,000. Well, the knife *did* have the original sheath to go with it.

Breaux and his roommate would practice *duel wielding* just to hone their skills, as actual fencing tournaments didn't include the two sword option.

The Bowie knife was about a foot long. He pulled it out of the case with his left hand and rotated his wrist. *This would work as a parrying dagger*, he thought.

Holding the weapons made him feel a little more secure. A portion of youthful exuberance must have simmered inside. Still, what could two primitive swords do to stop a raging dinosaur? Breaux had no desire to find out.

"Doc, what are you doing back there?" Bridget asked while standing next to Kathy and Dave.

Stinky was in the wheelbarrow. His arms and legs drooped over the bed nearly touching the floor.

He held up the two swords. "I'm going to borrow these."

Stepping toward him, Bridget said, "Really, Doc? A sword and a big knife?" She lowered her head and gazed questionably at him. "What do you plan on doing with those?"

"I don't *plan on* doing anything with them," Breaux said, not appreciating the tone. Bridget had come off as a brooding mother who didn't want her *little boy* to hurt himself. "We are leaving a perfectly secure place to *foolishly* risk our lives for one man." *Darn it!* Breaux had betrayed himself in front of the group. He had been keeping his feelings in check, but Bridget had pushed him too far.

Not wanting to start a debate on staying or going, Breaux continued, "If we are attacked, we have at least *something* besides our bare hands to defend ourselves." He then stepped from the back of the counter and headed toward the door.

Breaux peered through the front windows; shifting his gaze carefully around. "I don't see anything of concern out there now."

The wheel squeaked again as Dave pushed Stinky toward the front.

"Is he heavy?" Bridget asked.

"Not too," Dave said. "The wheelbarrow is sturdier than I thought it would be. I wish it had an inflatable tire instead of a solid one, though."

"If you get tired, I can take over," Bridget said.

Breaux looked at the portly man in the wheelbarrow. His heart sank a bit as Stinky simply looked pitiful. Another wave of regret washed over him for saying that trying to save the poor man was *foolish.*

"Are we good to go?" Kathy asked as she waited by the door.

"As near as I can tell," Breaux said.

Kathy twisted the thumbturn on the deadbolt.

The metallic click started the race.

The flight attendant exited first; with Dave close behind doing the heavy lifting.

Bridget followed, and Breaux pulled up the rear.

The street was deserted for at least a few blocks, though Breaux thought he saw cars ahead at an intersection.

The professor suddenly felt exposed, as if he were naked walking through a pit of vipers. There was an eerie background roar; screams, reptilian hiss-cries, and gunshots told the story that *the good times were not rolling anymore.*

"Those are police cars up there!" Bridget said with excitement in her voice.

They had passed an intersection without encountering any surprises. Just two more blocks to go. The incessant, cycling squeak from the wheelbarrow really pricked Breaux's nerves. It reminded him of a wounded bird just *begging* for a predator to find and eat it.

"Can you take over for a minute," Dave said to Bridget.

"Sure."

Dave stopped and set the wheelbarrow legs on the street. He flexed his arms and fingers, to get new blood circulating, and to loosen his tight muscles.

Bridget was a real trooper. She had Stinky up and rolling at a steady pace.

They were going to make it! One more block and a half and they would arrive at the line of police cars.

Breaux realized he had been running with a knife and a sword the whole time and thought of the old saying that *you shouldn't run with scissors.* He was such a *manly man* to live this dangerously. The thought made him smile. Soon, they would be in a safe place, and Stinky would get his life-saving insulin.

He needed to be protective of the two blades too. Replacing them would cost nearly $15,000. Now he felt a bit silly for taking the weapons in the first place. Really, what could *he* possibly have done to stop a raging dinosaur? He'd probably throw them down and run had they been attacked.

"I'll take back over," Dave said.

Bridget complied, and Dave powered the wheelbarrow once again.

As they crossed the next intersection, a young boy rounded the corner of a building, holding a tall bucket he probably used as a drum to perform street music for tips. It shocked Breaux when the boy's feet left the ground as a reptilian head lifted him by his shirt collar.

Dr. Bryan Breaux froze. A troodon had control of the boy and would soon eviscerate him.

The other three carried on down St. Peter; apparently so caught up in their flight they didn't notice the boy or dinosaur when they had passed.

He almost bolted after them.

But he couldn't.

The boy was too scared to scream, but he loudly whimpered in fear.

This was it. Breaux could either choose to live or risk dying right now.

Life would not be worth living with the memory of doing nothing to save an innocent child.

He yelled at the beast as a challenge.

"Dr. Breaux!" Bridget called, apparently she had heard him too.

"Keep going!" he yelled back. This was no time to endanger any more lives.

The troodon had taken note of the human who approached to take its prize. It widened its lips to expose teeth and hissed while keeping its hold on the boy.

As Breaux neared, the dinosaur turned around to flee with its food. The professor *flung* at the troodon; using a flying leap added speed and power to his saber's jab.

The blow struck haphazardly placed, but the blade pushed past skin on its back and hit bone.

The troodon snapped its head around and hissed again.

Its mouth empty, Breaux saw the boy picking himself off the ground.

"Run!" Breaux shouted.

He didn't have to give the warning twice. The boy left his bucket and tore down St. Peter Street. Breaux caught a glimpse of Bridget rushing to meet him before the troodon took its turn to attack.

The head on the long neck shot toward him. The dinosaur was too close to use his saber, so he brought the Bowie knife around and connected with the left side of its face. He did this while using a fencing move called the *passata sotto*, an evasive movement where he dropped his body below where teeth were intended to connect.

The knife blade bit deep into jaw and snout. The troodon backed away a few steps. Blood and slimy liquid dripped from its nose and mouth.

Having a momentary advantage, Breaux used a series of *feints* to confuse and attack the wounded dinosaur. His footwork was better than he thought after all those years since college. His swordsmanship too felt natural, despite the heavier saber.

The troodon tried once again to bite his head, but Breaux managed to dive to the side and hack into its neck where the blade cut halfway through.

The blow sent the troodon staggering.

This was no time to show quarter.

Breaux unleashed a *remise*, a short series of attacks where he at no time would withdraw his weapon.

The neck wound bled profusely. The jugular probably had been severed. Blood pooled so much under Breaux's feet he could hear it splash.

Now swaying like a sapling in a strong wind, Breaux performed his final *lunge* to the troodon's heart.

The dinosaur flopped onto the street. Its eyes glassy and void of life as they looked toward the sky.

Dr. Bryan Breaux had done the impossible. He had won.

Blood from the dinosaur stained the polished blade of the saber. He looked at it and remembered hearing stories of how hunters rubbed blood on a new hunter, after their first kill.

He brought the blade near his face and brushed it against both of his cheeks.

His chest swole as he thought of rescuing the boy. But then, he remembered how this whole mess was his fault. How many more young boys weren't saved today? How many people would die because of him?

He took a deep breath and let some of the burdens go. He had no idea the entangle experiment would go awry. The time shift was out of his control. A similar result was more than likely to happen when the Q device was used again. Still, he was the *catalyst* who ushered in this destruction. That was a fact he was just going to have to learn to live with. And, he vowed to use the gift of his second chance at life unselfishly and truly help others in need.

Shouts from up the street broke him from his reverie. He saw Bridget, Dave, Kathy, and the boy waving to him.

Breaux took one last look at the dead troodon and gave thanks that he was blessed to have won. He turned and trotted up the street to the welcoming cheers and slaps on the back from Bridget and his new friends. The boy ran over and hugged his leg.

Medical professionals had Stinky on a stretcher and attended to him.

"Doc, I had no idea you were such a swordsman," Bridget said, a smile stretched across her face.

"That was some great footwork you had out there," Dave said.

"Great job, Dr. Breaux. You're a hero," Kathy said.

Breaux looked at Bridget, knowing the irony of the situation. He would say nothing contrary, though.

"The police said the National Guard is on its way," Bridget said. "They're escorting people in groups to the Super Dome. Come on, there's another group going soon, and we can go with them."

The professor looked down into the face of the boy who still clutched his leg. "Hey, little man. You ready to leave and go to the Super Dome?"

"Are the Saints playing?" the boy innocently asked.

Breaux laughed. "No, not today, but someone will be there who will help you find your parents."

"Shucks, that's too bad. I've never seen the Saints play a football game."

Taking a knee and matching gazes with the boy, Breaux said, "Tell you what, the next game the Saints play in the Super Dome, I'll take you and your family."

"You will? For real?" the boy said with delight.

"Yep, and I'll buy you all the popcorn and candy your parents will allow."

"Thanks, I can hardly wait!'

"Me too," Breaux said and patted the boy on his shoulder. "Me too," he said to himself, hoping and praying that returning to normal life was even possible.

CHAPTER 11

Doing his best not to call any attention to himself, Broderick Brown reached under his shirt and came out with his pistol. He wished he would have told T-Bob, the zoo employee, he had a gun earlier, but there wasn't an opportunity. Hopefully, the man wouldn't freak out when he saw it.

T-Bob had them out of sight of the two dinosaurs for a brief minute, but then Broderick saw the prehistoric creatures following their trail, sniffing the air, and looking about.

Then, one deinonychus locked its gaze on the small group and hissed with a wide opened mouth. It charged forward, and the other one quickly followed.

"Run! We've got to run!" Broderick yelled.

No one questioned his command, and the four took out running as fast as their legs would churn.

"How far, T-Bob? How far?" Broderick asked.

"The reptile house is close to the river. We might not make it in time," T-Bob said.

The deinonychuses had cut the distance between them in half. If they got too close, Broderick would have to stop and start shooting. It would buy his family extra time, but he didn't know if it would be enough for them to get away. "Is there someplace closer?"

"The cats! The big cats are right over there!" T-Bob said and veered to his right toward the lion exhibit.

The zoo employee led them down a small walk, behind the lion enclosure, to an eight-foot-wide opening.

Broderick had lost sight of the dinosaurs before they entered the dark hallway.

"Whew." By the smell of things, there was no doubt there were big cats nearby. He wondered how the dinosaurs would react to the felines. Hopefully, the cats would have their attention and would forget about him and his family.

They came next to a cage door and stopped.

"Open the door, and let's go in," Broderick said, wondering why T-Bob stood with his nose between the door bars.

"Can't. The cats aren't put up," T-Bob said.

About that time, a male lion sauntered toward the door. It was a beautiful animal. Its mane adorned its big head making it four times larger. Its tongue hung down as it panted. When it lifted its upper lip, there were teeth capable of shredding a man to pieces in a matter of minutes.

"This is *Harvey*," T-Bob said. He put the back of his hand by the cage, and the lion came up and gave it a sniff. "I'm friends with all the animals here. Even the hippo, but he still throws poop on me from time to time and laughs."

"So, what? Are we trapped here? What if—?" Broderick's words caught in his throat when he saw the head of one of the dinosaurs sniff around the entrance. At least the hallway was dark, but he had no idea how keen the dinosaur's eyesight was.

To his relief, the first dinosaur moved out of sight, but shortly after the other came into the entrance and sniffed around.

By this time, another male lion had joined alongside Harvey, and two females slowly approached. The cats might have thought it was snack time, but Broderick wondered if they were anticipating one human each for a meal.

The deinonychus poked its head forward and hissed. The other came back into view.

"They know we're here," Broderick said. He turned on the laser and pointed his weapon.

T-Bob gasped, and said, "You gotta gun? You can't have a gun at the zoo."

"Cool it, T-Bob. We don't have any other choice. We're trapped, and it's the only way out," Broderick said.

"Maybe not," T-Bob said.

Broderick didn't have time to waste playing twenty questions with the zoo employee. The two dinosaurs looked like they were getting ready to charge, and he had to make his shots count.

Keys jingled behind him. Then a mechanical *clank* and the moan of rusty hinges told Broderick T-Bob had opened the gate to the lions.

"Get behind the gate!" T-Bob yelled as he pulled the gate toward them. The barred barrier shielded them from the opening to the lions' enclosure.

"T-Bob, are you nuts?" Broderick cried out as the gate swung around and hit him in the shoulder, pushing him back against the wall.

The lions wasted no time charging down the hall. Their roars echoing as the deinonychuses backed up in uncertainty.

One deinonychus made a clean exit, but the first male lion that came upon the other slapped it with its mighty paw, and knocked it backward into the clear.

The deinonychus reared its head back and attempted to bite the lion's neck—teeth snapped at empty air.

The other male lion sprang from, what looked like to Broderick, ten feet away. The lion landed on the dinosaur's chest, bringing it to the ground.

The female lions exited the entrance, and a few seconds later, Broderick saw them tag-teaming the other dinosaur.

"Can we go in the lion cage now?" Broderick asked T-Bob.

"No, there're two more inside. Those cats are old and sleep a lot. We need to leave while we can," T-Bob said.

"Past them fighting out there?" Dionne asked.

As crazy as it sounded, they had to take the best of the few choices available. "We've got to make a try," Broderick said. "Follow me."

The big man helped push the cage door closed, and T-Bob locked it. Then, he quickly led the other three down the hall to the entrance.

It was four on two. The dinosaurs held their own, but they certainly looked worse for wear.

Not only were dinosaurs roaming about, but now four lions would be on the loose too. Broderick wanted to get away from this whole place as soon as possible. Then, a thought occurred to him. He looked at his watch, and said, "T-Bob, the streetcar comes by here at the top of the hour, right?"

"Yeah."

"Can you get us there in fifteen minutes?"

"No problem. It's over by the levee."

"Okay, girls. Follow T-Bob, and I'll pull up the rear," Broderick said.

The last glimpse before they turned a corner informed him the male lions had taken down their adversary, enjoying the spoils of the kill. It looked like the females fared well enough to enjoy dinner too.

Several minutes had passed with no surprises holding them back. The few people he had seen fleeing were heading toward the front. He thought about shouting and telling them their plan to take a streetcar out of there. But what if he would have led them to their deaths? He had no idea if this plan would work. He gambled with the life of his family. He couldn't bring himself to lead others into an uncertain fate.

They ran past the elephant fountain, the Louisiana swamp, Jaguar Jungle, and neared the Rhino Range. The streetcar wasn't far from that.

Broderick looked at his watch. There was plenty of time to make it to the streetcar. In fact, now that they were at the Rhino Range, he could see the streetcar arrival/departure station.

There was only one problem. When Broderick saw it, goosebumps popped up on his arms.

A dinosaur much bigger than the other two they had encountered loomed by a cluster of trees between them and the station. "Stop!" Broderick called out.

T-Bob and the girls lifted their weary gazes off the ground and over to him.

He pointed toward the station. "Look, by those trees. It's a dinosaur, and that sucker is big." Over ten feet tall, if Broderick had to guess. Still, it was smaller than what he thought a T. rex would be. But what did he know about dinosaurs other than what movies like Jurassic Park had taught him? "We'll have to go another way."

"There *is* no other way," T-Bob said. "Oh no, he sees us!"

Looking around the area, there was no secure place to shelter. Broderick didn't think bullets from his gun would do much to stop a behemoth like that. He needed a big game rifle or a RPG. "Everyone, listen to me. Run away now. I'm staying and will slow it down."

"But—" Dionne started.

"No time to argue," Broderick said. He turned his gaze to Dionne. "I'm sorry for everything. I love you." He turned to Keesha, and said, "Keesha, Daddy loves you. I'll always love you."

"I love you, Daddy," Keesha said as tears rolled down her face.

"T-Bob? What are you doing? Get my girls out of here!" Brodrick said as he turned his gaze to find the zoo employee by a gate.

"Get over here and help me open the emergency exit," T-Bob said.

Before he asked *why*, Broderick's gaze fixated on the approaching white rhinoceros.

The beast was as large as a truck and surely weighed as much. It trotted over toward T-Bob as he struggled to pull the gate open. It had a stout, pointed horn at the end of its elongated head that looked like it could puncture battleship steel.

"Come help me with the gate," T-Bob cried again. "Grass has grown up over the bottom."

Broderick pulled Dionne and Keesha over with him. The dinosaur had picked up its pace. All three helped the zoo employee pull the gate free.

The rhino gave them a leary eye as they hid behind the gate and it stepped out to freedom.

The dilophosaurus' roaring hiss did nothing to frighten the rhino. It must have taken the battle cry as a challenge to its territory. The rhino lowered its massive head and grunted like a bull. Then, it made a muffled trumpet-like sound—something like the mix of an elephant and killer whale.

It grunted a few more times and lifted its long head up and down, jabbing the thick, protruding horn toward the sky. Its wide, padded feet reminded Broderick of outriggers on a truck crane. The rhino started a slow trot toward the charging dinosaur.

Broderick watched in amazement as the hulking beast gained speed. With surprising grace, the animal looked like it was running near thirty miles-an-hour!

Turning his head, thinking they might need to reconsider the streetcar and head all the way back to the front, Broderick saw a few unidentifiable dinosaurs lurking about on the path they took to get there. His plan had been a gamble from the onset, but now there were no other options. He was all in, and he had bet the lives of those he loved most.

The rhino sped like a locomotive toward the dinosaur, huffing its grunts, and leading with the wicked weapon growing from its nose.

The dilophosaurus leaned its head forward; its back parallel to the ground as its legs traveled wide spans, making it look over twenty feet long. As it neared, a pair of bright red, rounded crests on its skull came into view that ran all the way to its nose.

The two creatures collided without either showing quarter.

Broderick heard the impact before the savage cry of the dinosaur followed.

The rhino's momentum came to a screeching halt.

The dinosaur's chest took the brunt of the impact. Its neck came down abruptly, and its jaw smashed against the rhino's back.

With the rhino having a clear advantage, Broderick hurried T-Bob and his family from behind the gate and led the way to the streetcar, as rhino and dinosaur battled it out.

The dilophosaurus had rolled off the rhino's horn and laid on its side. But before the rhino went in for another skewer to finish the job, the dinosaur swung its neck and tail about like a catfish out of the water in the bottom of a boat.

The dilophosaurus' tail slapped the rhino on the side, which made enough impact for it to stumble a few feet sideways, but that was about it.

Coming to its feet, the dinosaur had some obvious difficulty solidifying its balance. Still, it lashed out with an open mouth. The dilophosaurus' teeth contacted the back of the rhino's head. The dinosaur's mouth wasn't wide enough, nor its teeth long and sharp enough, to maintain a grip.

The rhino shook the dinosaur's bite away by jerking its head toward it and bringing its horn under the adversary's neck, leaving a cut that immediately dripped red.

Broderick was amazed that his wife and daughter could tune out the savagery as they ran past. The beasts weren't a hundred feet away; much too close for comfort!

He saw the streetcar had not made it to the depot. "What time is it?" he called out to T-Bob.

Between breaths, T-Bob said, "My watch says twelve-oh-five."

Well, that's not good. Broderick thought the streetcar should be there now.

The dilophosaurus cried out again unlike before. The rhino had the dinosaur on its back, and the white beast pushed its horn past ribs as it powered its way forward. Once again, Mother Earth's present children claimed victory over those from the prehistoric past.

The depot was empty. When Broderick turned and looked down the tracks, he saw what he believed to be the streetcar. It was hard to tell because of the distance.

After looking in every direction, the Mississippi River several hundred feet away with no means to navigate, the only practical choice available was to head east toward the vehicle.

After a few moments of catching their breaths, Broderick said, "We have to keep going...follow the tracks to the streetcar."

"The streetcar's not moving. Do you think it's broken?" Dionne asked.

"I hope not. I don't know what's wrong, but we can't go west, the river curves north and that puts us back to the front of the zoo. We can't swim the river. This is our only choice," Broderick said, thinking how his limited options of late were bound to put him in an unwinnable situation.

"Keesha, you can do this, right?" Broderick asked.

She nodded and fluffed the braids off the back of her neck.

Broderick noticed how Keesha looked so grown up right then. Nothing like his little girl that served him tea in her plastic cups along with cardboard cookies he pretended to eat. Now he feared he wouldn't get to see her grow old enough to drive a car...graduate college...get married and have children.

"We need to go if we're going," T-Bob said.

"Stay together. T-Bob, you lead."

The zoo employee did as instructed. Dionne and Keesha picked up the pace. Broderick once again ran flank.

The journey took longer than Broderick had expected. The streetcar was over a mile away. His imagination ran wild, watching the wooded area that ran parallel to the tracks, thinking he saw a dinosaur waiting to spring out and attack.

He heard each breath Dionne and Keesha took. If they didn't find shelter soon, he didn't know how much longer they could hold out. Heck, he didn't know how much longer *he* could hold out. The stress wore him down as much as the physical activity.

As the streetcar came into focus, it was obvious why it was dead on the tracks. There were several dinosaurs, Keesha had called troodons, under the wheels preventing it from moving forward.

Not only that, but a few partially consumed human bodies laid on the ground to either side of the rail.

"Hold up," Broderick called out.

Everyone trotted to a halt.

Stepping to the lead position, Broderick had his gun held out in front and scanned the area for any signs of dinosaurs. He couldn't see inside the streetcar or in front of it. For now, it looked as if the beasts that committed this calamity had moved on.

"Dionne, don't let Keesha see this," Broderick said.

Dionne nodded, and said, "Keesha, baby. Just keep your eyes on the ground when we walk to the streetcar."

"Let's go," Broderick said.

When they were thirty or so feet away from the streetcar, Broderick held them back as he made a fast dash to check inside.

His stomach roiled as he passed mangled bodies. Gruesome wounds in soft flesh exposed bones and internal organs. Death stares etched onto innocent faces recorded unimaginable horrors.

To his relief, the streetcar's doors were open and nothing of danger lurked inside, other than what blood had contaminated. There were two mangled bodies near the back of an older man and woman.

Broderick dragged them both outside and wondered if they were husband and wife. Such a pity they had lived to an old age for it to come to an end so violently.

Wiping his hands on his pants, he motioned the others to get aboard.

Bloodstains streaked down the side of the streetcar. As near as Broderick could tell, once the vehicle came to a stop, dinosaurs tall enough pulled passengers out through the windows. For whatever reason, instead of closing the windows and waiting things out, the doors were opened and those who thought fleeing was the best option, did so. That proved to be a bad idea. But he knew when people panicked, *rationality* became a precious commodity.

"There's a lot of blood in there. Try not to touch any of it," Broderick said as Dionne led Keesha up the steps.

"Dinosaurs killed all these people?" T-Bob asked.

"I don't know what else to think," Broderick said.

"Do you know how to drive a streetcar?"

"Yeah, it's not that hard. I used to sit up front whenever I could as a kid and watched the driver. Sometimes the driver would show me how to operate the controls."

"Don't we have to move the dinosaurs out from under the wheels so we can go to the depot and turn around?"

"We don't have to turn around," Broderick said. "Climb in, and I'll show you."

Dionne and Keesha sat near the front on a twin seat. Keesha had her head snuggly in Dionne's protective embrace.

"See this switch?" Broderick pointed to a round green flange with a square head protruding in the middle. A wrench hung from a chain right next to it. He picked up the wrench and turned the square head. "Now we can travel in reverse."

Dionne's large brown eyes gazed back at him. Broderick wanted to tell her *not to worry*, and that *things would be okay*. But the last thing he wanted to do now was promise her something he might not be able to deliver.

Words meant nothing.

Action meant life or death.

It was up to him to make things right.

"T-Bob, close all the windows," Broderick said.

The streetcar was short enough where he could see out of the back. Broderick grabbed the accelerator handle and adjusted the brake lever.

The streetcar hummed to life, and the four headed down the bank of the Mississippi toward the French Quarter.

Dionne's cell phone rang. She pulled it from her pocket, and said, "It's my dad."

Answering, she said, "Yes, Daddy. I'm okay. We're all okay. Broderick is with us. We were at the zoo."

Her face went blank as she listened in silence. She moved the phone away from her mouth, and said to Broderick, "Dinosaurs are in the French Quarter too. Daddy's hurt and hiding in Saint Louis Cathedral."

She returned to the phone conversation, "We're on a streetcar heading that way.We don't have any choice. Dinosaurs attacked at the zoo too. I—"

Dionne looked at Broderick. "Lost connection. Daddy said he was safe. We're on the way to the French Quarter now. We have to find him and hide out until we're rescued."

At least before Broderick believed he had a chance to be free from prehistoric predators. Now, he was on a path leading them to more of the same. His only choice was to jump from one fire into another.

Luck had finally run out.

CHAPTER 12

The giganotosaurus in the center of Jackson Square roared with a cry that sounded like a snake hiss through a tuba amplified by deep bass subwoofers, when it slammed its head and body into the General Jackson statue.

The twenty-thousand-pound memorial shattered into mostly large pieces. Some smaller chunks shot out like shrapnel, hitting Andrew Jackson and Rev. Martin Scott on the back of their legs as they fled toward the sanctuary of St. Louis Cathedral.

Andrew had Scott's right arm around his neck, doing his best to support the protest leader's weight. Perspiration dripping down the man's face wet his left shoulder. With each step, Scott felt a little heavier.

A piece of the statue slid under Andrew's right foot and the concrete sidewalk—almost sending both tumbling to the ground. He managed to regain his footing, only to look to his left and see another danger streaking toward them.

This dinosaur had light blue feathers on its lizard-like head and small arms. Its neck was short, unlike the troodons that attacked others in the crowd. Though not as tall, the aura projected by this creature made Andrew feel helpless as a mouse about to be pounced on by a Siberian tiger.

"Reverend!" one of the leader's supporters yelled and zipped across their path to engage the dinosaur.

The supporter held nunchakus in his right hand and swung the hardwood clubs connected to a short chain above his head.

The velociraptor looked like a blue demon as it went in for the kill.

Nunchakus swiped through the air where the dinosaur had been.

The creature moved too fast for the unfortunate supporter. It leaped through the air with its clawed feet spread wide and stuck to his chest.

The man screamed and dropped his weapon—grabbing the dinosaur with both of his hands and desperately trying to rip the beast free.

The attempt was futile. Even though the velociraptor was less than half the man's weight, he couldn't pry it off for a chance to escape.

The deadly dinosaur proceeded to bite off chunks of flesh from the supporter's face. The velociraptor had no sense of mercy and ate its victim alive.

The clash had started and ended in a blink of an eye. Andrew caught it all before he and Scott reached the three-tiered water fountain they had to pass before arriving at the black iron gates leading out of Jackson Square.

The giganotosaurus roared again. Thankfully, it sounded like it took a different path toward the river.

From Andrew's estimation, the number of warriors had thinned greatly. He hoped most had found safe refuge, but his eyes told him many lost their lives today; their bodies desecrated as vicious teeth stripped flesh from bone and entered the bellies of the savage victors.

The two stepped out of Jackson Square and onto Chartres Street. Orange plastic fencing walled off a section of the street undergoing renovation.

Andrew looked from side to side and didn't see a soul. A three-piece band had abandoned their instruments. Artists had left their masterpieces hanging from the iron fence surrounding the Square. Tables with Tarot cards and chess boards with matches unfinished waited for their owners to return. A discarded drink and ice cream cart held treasures that Andrew thought might soon become more valuable than gold.

St. Louis Cathedral's white façade beckoned with its gates open leading to the humble brown stained double doors. Standing in its presence made Andrew feel he was in the courtyard of Heaven, and the Almighty was right there on the throne.

The Cathedral had a towering center spire and two smaller spires on each side. Viewed from Jackson Square, with the statue of Andrew Jackson in the foreground, the two images were the most closely associated with New Orleans.

With the statue gone, New Orleans would never be the same.

"Hang in there," Andrew said as they made it across the street.

Coming to the double doors, Andrew pushed with no reward for his effort. His heart sank to his stomach. A quick look around provided many options, but he didn't know what might be open. With Scott's condition worsening, he couldn't afford to make wrong decisions.

"Anybody in there?" Andrew yelled as he pounded on the door.

Rev. Scott heaved for air. His eyelids hung weakly like half-open shades.

The door miraculously pulled open. "Quick!" a man at the door said.

Andrew lowered his head and half-dragged Rev. Scott into the lobby.

Inside, to the right, a large number of lit candles arranged on votive stands burned as offerings for special blessings. A brightly colored statue of the Blessed Mother cast her watchful gaze over it to welcome Parishioners in need.

A chandelier hung overhead, casting dim yellow lighting between the front doors and entrance to the nave, where the worshipers would sit.

A sign pointed to the left showing the way to the gift shop.

Easing Rev. Scott to the floor, Andrew looked about and counted four men sizing them up.

Three were members of the Sons of the Confederacy; identified by *The Blood-Stained Banner* flag of the Confederate States of America on their caps. The white stars and blue crossbars on the red background inspired pride and triggered hatred of millions over the last one hundred and fifty years.

The other man wore navy colored pants and shirt with a patch on a shoulder sporting the Odal rune. It was obvious he was a card-carrying member of the National Socialist Movement. The scowl on his face let Andrew know he wasn't impressed with the present company.

Turning his attention to Rev. Scott, he said, "How bad is your knee?"

The protest leader looked relieved to be sitting down. He had his legs stretched out in front of him and his palms on the checkered black and white tile just behind his back to help prop himself up. "Something's torn in my knee, for sure." He lifted his gaze and smoothed the pain from his face. "I'll heal," he said as if his will was stronger than the injury.

"I'll try to make you as comfortable as I can until we can get you help," Andrew said.

Rev. Scott smirked. "Don't worry about me. I'm cool."

"Why are you guys in the lobby and not inside the church?" Andrew asked the four men.

"Entrance doors are locked solid. The gift shop too. I guess the priests don't want any of their stuff destroyed or stolen," one of the Sons of the Confederacy, the older of the three members there, said.

"Was that true what you said to that reporter? You're a descendant of General Jackson?" the man asked.

Andrew lifted himself off one knee and rose. "Yes, it's true. I can trace my ancestry back to the General."

"That fact won't get you any special privileges in this town," Rev. Scott said. "Not anymore."

"I don't recall asking for any *special privileges*," Andrew said and wondered why the protest leader bothered to waste the energy to continue the conflict. Nothing would get resolved with more pressing questions like *How are we going to get out of here alive?* facing them.

"I do find that fact interesting," the older man said. "My name's *Randy Guillaume*. These are my two nephews, Doug," he pointed to a thirty-something-year-old man with a red beard, "and Tim," a skinny younger man who wore braces.

"Why did you bring that *filth* in here with you?" the NSM member asked. His hair buzzed so short it looked like someone had outlined it on his head with a brown marker.

"Yep, just like I thought. *Wecolme to the party*," Rev. Scott said. "Why don't you white boys talk about your four-wheel-drive trucks. I'm going to call my daughter," Rev. Scott said while digging out his phone from his front pocket.

Getting lumped in the same category as a white supremacist chapped Andrew's backside. Now wasn't the time or place to make a plea for Rev. Scott to differentiate his position from the others. "You know, that was uncalled for," he said to the NSM member.

"That's where you're wrong," the NSM member said. "It's people like him that divide the nation—make us weak. The fact that you stand up for him is part of the nation's problem today. White people like you make us weaker."

"Hold on there, young fella," Randy said. "All lives are sacred in God's eyes. You can't choose to let people die because of their race or that they believe something different. That's not Christian."

"I'm an Atheist. I don't care about God. If this nation is to survive, we need to have a union of white people to form a greater America," the NSM member said. "So it doesn't matter if we lose someone not of pure white blood."

"Heck, boy, I don't know how you would go about determining who had *pure white blood* and who didn't. Everybody has the same color blood. *Red*, like the background of this flag," Randy said and pointed to the Confederate flag on his hat. "The Sons of the Confederacy aren't trying to take away anyone's rights. We just want to have *equal rights*. We're proud of our heritage, and we want it preserved. That's the American way."

Doug and Tim stood quietly by; turning their attention to each speaker like they were watching a tennis match.

Scott spoke to someone on his phone; presumably his daughter.

"Only whites should be members of the nation. Only members of the nation can be citizens of the state. The right to vote belongs to white people. All non-whites are guests in this country and should abide by different laws," the NSM member said.

"I've heard about enough," Andrew said. "This isn't a National Socialist Movement rally. And for the life of me, I don't understand how anyone can take such an extreme position as you do."

"Darn! Lost my connection," Rev. Scott said in the background.

"Yeah. The Sons of Confederacy want to stay away as far as possible from a bunch of Nazis. We're nothing alike," Randy said.

"I don't know, Unc," Doug said. "I kinda like the idea of an *all-white* America."

"And the truth will *set you free*," Rev. Scott interrupted and struggled to rise to his feet. His sentiments about race relations in America just reinforced.

CHAPTER 13

Jacob Poche fled the Southern Queen's promenade deck like his feet were on fire as the massive squid's feeding tentacle came back up over the railing. He sailed into Eric Lott, a fellow member of Sigma Nu at UL Lafayette, and both tumbled down into the Creole Room on the middle deck.

Jacob had so much adrenaline surging through his body he felt as if ants crawled over his skin. Death had never been that close before. And what almost killed him? A giant squid! Really? Jacob had a history of bad luck following him, but this was ridiculous.

Concerned people in the room helped Jacob and Eric to their feet and asked if they were hurt.

The two waved them off, and their attention drew to others who stood near the north windows.

"Oh no! It's got another one," a short-haired woman said.

The giant squid held Jacob's savior in the air near its mouth. It looked as if it was toying with him.

"He's not going down without a fight. Hit him! Hit him with the ax!" Eric said while raising a fist and striking air.

After a few errant swings, the ax slipped from the man's grasp and plunged into the water.

"Oh, he's toast now," Eric said.

Jacob was powerless to do anything but watch. That could be him right now—hanging in the air about to be eaten by a monster from a nightmare.

More people gasped, and one man whimpered that he *couldn't look*.

The squid bit off the man's legs at the knees, and his upper body fell free of the tentacle and splashed in the river.

Surprisingly, the man had enough life left in him to attempt an escape. He stretched out his arms and swam, slightly pulling away from the squid.

"Look at 'im! The current's helping him get away," Eric said. "Go! Go! Go!"

Jacob realized Eric had no concept of what the poor man faced. This was no video game or SYFY Channel movie. Although, he was just as guilty as his frat brother in the *naïve department* in this case. When he spotted the giant squid, if he had gone down to the next deck instead of getting a better view of it, the man probably would be standing right by them rather than seconds away from death.

"He's going to get away," the short-haired woman said with eagerness in her voice.

The man had made it about twenty feet from the creature when the feeding tentacle rose from under the water and blocked his swim path.

"Oh no!" a man said.

"Shoot...it's pulling him back toward its mouth," Eric said.

"Just let the poor man die..." Jacob said to himself. He felt the despair of the soon to be dead hero.

"I know what that squid is doing," Eric said. "It's acting like a cat. You ever see a cat catch a small animal and play with it a while before it kills it?"

The tentacle had the man up in the air and heading for the squid's beak. The cruel game was finally coming to an end.

The beak opened and wolfed down its latest victim.

"Aw, dude...tough break," Eric said.

Jacob's shoulders sagged. It hurt being alive right now—feeling like it was he who had committed the death. "I...I don't even know his name."

"It's coming for the boat!" the short-haired woman yelled.

The squid had its feeding tentacles reaching out for the boat as its mantle traveled smoothly through the water. The one eye grew larger as it approached, reminding Jacob of a new moon on a cloudless night.

The crowd in the room swayed off balance as the boat succumbed to the sea monster's clutches.

"Man, it's trying to sink the boat. That's messed up," Eric said.

Some of the squid's eight legs contacted the boat's bow. The soft roar of the engine grew as the load on the paddlewheel increased.

"It's going to sink us!" an old man cried out. "We're all going to die."

"I don't want to get eaten by the monster," a little girl told her mother.

A window shattered on the opposite side of the room. Jacob turned and saw a man-sized, triangular-shaped reptilian head push past the broken glass. The creature opened its mouth, revealing rows of sharp fangs.

Shrieks and screams from scattering passengers did nothing to frighten the beast away. The head pivoted on a long neck, and its jaws closed on an unfortunate man who had slipped during his haphazard escape.

The man yelled so intensely that Jacob's ears rang.

There was no helping the victim, as the elasmosaur's head retreated from the window with jaws holding tightly to its squirming prize.

"What the heck was that?" Eric asked. "Man, things are sure getting weird around here."

That was a real understatement, Jacob thought. The boat listed further. He didn't know if that was because of the squid's pull or because of the shifting weight of the mass of people in the Creole Room pushing their way to the stairs leading to the first deck.

Another window shattered, and more screams rose, but it didn't happen on the second deck.

Jacob thought a second, and said, "It's attacking the first deck now. There's no safe place to hide. We've got to do something."

"Swim for shore?" Eric said.

"No, *genius*. We've got to figure a way out of this mess," Jacob said.

"What can we do? We're just a couple of college kids."

"Which means we ought to have the brains to do something."

"Like what?"

Jacob looked around the room as frightened people made their way back up to the second deck. The bar had plenty of liquor to make Molotov cocktails, but the last thing he wanted to do was accidentally start a fire aboard the boat. Plus, the creatures were in the water and could easily submerge to extinguish the flame. "We need a gun...or a bomb."

"If we had some sparklers, we could wrap them together with tape and make a bomb," Eric said.

"Yeah, that's a great idea. But I don't think the boat carries any fireworks." What would they have on the boat regarding emergency equipment? Jacob thought. Then, it hit him, "I've got it. Flares! I bet they have flares. We have to go upstairs to the helm and look for flares."

Jacob didn't wait for Eric to respond. He didn't care if his frat mate was coming along or not, and he certainly wasn't going to waste any time discussing it with him.

Still, he felt relieved when he heard the second pair of shoes hit the stairs and he neared the promenade deck.

Jacob put on the brakes as soon as he reached the third deck. The giant squid was port side. Its eye hovered above the railing looking as big as a freight truck. Its feeding tentacles had a firm hold on the bow.

Eric stopped right behind him. "Wh—, oh man...look at that." He rubbed his hand through his hair. "What do we do now? Do you want to run past it?"

Not liking the consequences of guessing wrong, spotting a fire hose on a reel gave Jacob new inspiration. "I've got it! We'll use the high-pressure fire hose to drive it away."

"You think that'll work?"

Jacob had made the mistake of attending a protest where things got slightly out of hand. He had challenged the full force of a fire nozzle and lost miserably. "Let's hope so."

The hose reel was a few steps away over by the empty fire ax box. Jacob ran and grabbed the nozzle. Then, ran back, unreeling the hose.

He stood with the nozzle in his hands and realized the hose needed charging. Looking back at the reel, he saw a couple of unmarked levers near the deck. Jacob hollered to Eric, "We need to charge the pump! Go turn those levers over there." He pointed quickly with his left hand and then returned it to the nozzle.

"Which one?" Eric said on arrival.

"I don't know. Do both!"

Eric turned each lever and a pump motor engaged.

The flat hose swole. All that high-pressure water made the hose weigh down like filling it with concrete. Jacob pulled back on the bale handle. The nozzle burped air and shot out a wide fan of water. The pressure surge knocked Jacob slightly off balance, and he had to shuffle his feet and lean his weight toward the nozzle to stabilize. "Come give me a hand."

Eric sidled behind him and grabbed hold of the hose.

"You've got to lean into it. I'm going to narrow the water pattern," Jacob said.

Foam rolled out the nozzle, covering the deck. One of those levers must have activated fire foam to the hose.

"Hey! What are you kids doing down there?" a voice yelled from the observation deck.

It should have been blatantly obvious what they were doing. Trying to get the ship free of a sea monster!

Jacob twisted the fire nozzle. The water pattern shifted from a wide fan into a powerful stream.

The two walked forward, and Jacob aimed the stream right into the giant squid's eye.

Immediately, the beast shuddered and let out an otherworldly cry.

Jacob half expected to feel the blunt trauma from a flying tentacle but was rewarded with the squid's mantle disappearing under the water, taking its legs and feeding tentacles with it.

The Southern Queen righted itself, and the paddlewheel churned the mighty Mississippi once again.

"Great job, fellas!" the voice from the observation deck called down. "I can't believe that actually worked."

Jacob pushed the bale handle forward, slowly cutting off the water. He and Eric both stumbled forward and let the hose drop from their hold.

Looking up, Jacob saw it was one of the sailors who spoke to them. "Do you have any flares aboard?"

"Yeah, but we don't need flares. The captain radioed the Coast Guard, and they are on the way. We can probably make it to shore before they get here, thanks to you two."

"There's another monster attacking the passengers on the other side of the boat. There's no telling how many will die before then," Jacob said. "I have a plan to use flares to stop it."

After a few moments of hesitation, the sailor said, "Come on up."

Jacob switched the pump and foam levers back to the *off* position, as he and Eric passed to go to the door leading up to the helm and observation deck.

The sailor greeted them when they reached the top. "They're over here." He stepped over to a narrow closet and unlocked the door and opened it. "Top shelf."

There were six yellow flares about a foot long each. Jacob grabbed three and gave them to Eric, and then he took the other three. "Can you hold all of these together?" he asked Eric.

"I think so," Eric said. He took the other three flares and held them in a bundle.

"What'cha got in mind, boy?" the sailor asked.

Jacob picked up a roll of black electrical tape off a shelf. "You ever make a sparkler bomb?"

The sailor said, "No."

"If you wrap a box of sparklers with tape and leave one sticking out like a fuse and light it, when that one sparkler reaches the others, they'll go off like a bomb." Jacob proceeded to peel up the edge of electrical tape off the roll and wrap it around the flares. "I've never tried to do that with flares, but I'm hoping it works the same."

Jacob went round and round with the tape, wrapping the bundle as tightly as possible.

"Uh, Jacob?" Eric said.

"What?"

"I don't think this will work."

Stopping and directing his gaze from his efforts to Eric, Jacob said, "Why not?"

"Sparklers are basically wires dipped in a combustible coating made of gunpowder and metals. The outside of the sparkler burns. So, when you wrap them in tape and the fuse sparkler reaches the surrounding sparklers, they ignite. Then those sparklers ignite the ones touching it. It's that rapid release of energy that turns the sparklers into a bomb."

"And?"

"Jacob, these flares have paper casings on the outside. The pyrophoric material is on the inside. There won't be a rapid release of energy to make the flares explode like sparklers," Eric said.

"That makes sense," the sailor said. "You'll have one big flare, but you won't have a bomb."

Jacob thought a moment. "Okay, we'll use a great big flare to get rid of that monster."

"What are we going to do? Drop the flare on it and burn a hole through it?" Eric asked.

"I doubt if that would work. The flare would just bounce off of it and fall into the river," Jacob said.

"Then, what?"

Jacob smiled, and said, "We'll have to convince it to *come and get it.*"

*

When the three entered the Creole room, the passengers seeking refuge had used the tables and chairs to build a protective wall around themselves.

Glass covered a good portion of the floor from multiple broken windows. Wide swaths of blood smeared across the wooden planks and stained ornate rugs.

"Come hide with us, or you'll get killed," a concerned passenger called out.

A window shattered on the deck below, and a woman's shriek of terror announced the clasmosaur had claimed another victim.

"We can't waste any more time," Jacob said. He took the bundle of flares from Eric and bent close to the floor. He had left the center flare poking from the middle of the bundle because he planned to use it for a fuse. With that strategy abandoned, he had to make the flare ends even.

Tamping the protruding flare against the floor, he said, "We don't want one of them sticking out." After a few firm plants against the hard deck, he said, "There, it's ready to go."

"What next?" Eric asked.

"Simple. You're going to stick your arms and head out of a window and gets its attention," Jacob said.

"Like *heck* I am!" Eric said as if that was the dumbest thing he had ever heard in his life.

"You've got to act as bait. I'll take it from there," Jacob said.

"I don't think—"

"Just get its attention and then run to the other side of the room. It's no big deal. I'm taking all the risks," Jacob said.

"I'll do it," the sailor said.

"No, I'll do it," Eric said. "When we get out of this jam, Jacob's not going to tell anyone I chickened out. Besides," he paused, "Jacob's taking *all the risks*, right?"

Touché, Jacob thought. It was time to put the money where his mouth was.

Turning to the sailor, Jacob said, "How do we light these?"

The sailor reached his hand out and peeled a strip of paper from around the end of one flare. Then, he pulled a one-inch section off the end and held the bottom side up. "See that? That's the cap, and the bottom has a coarse striking surface similar to a book of matches. You light the flare like you would a match." He motioned the bottom of the cap above the end of the flare.

"Okay, let's do this," Jacob said.

The sailor peeled off the paper strips of the remaining flares and removed the caps.

Turning to Eric, he said, "Get into position."

Eric took a deep breath and turned his gaze toward the center window. With his neck stretched to the limit, he began a cautious approach.

"See anything yet?" Jacob asked as his friend was within arm's reach of his destination.

"No," Eric said, stepping as softly as he could. His body language indicated he would be ready to bolt for safety at the first sign of danger. He eased closer and stopped. "Hmm, nothing right now." He poked his head past to where the window glass should have been and looked to his left and right. "No—wait. I see something floating to the surface." He pulled his head away from exposure, turned, and pressed his back against the section of wall between the windows. "That thing is *big*. It's totally *huge*, dude."

"Time to light up," Jacob said. He held the flare bundle away from his body.

The sailor rubbed the cap bottom on the middle flare. After a few errant sparks, the flare lit brightly like a kitchen match. The molten material spewing out lit the other flares in a roaring display of pyrotechnics.

Jacob pointed the hot flare bundle at an angle to keep the sparks away from his face. "Eric, go dangle your worm out the window."

"What?"

"Stick your head out and call it. You're the bait."

Eric's body leaned forward a little then retracted at a steady even pace. It looked like he was counting; trying to build enough nerve to do the deed.

On the fifth nod of his head, he stuck his upper body out of the window and waved his hands wildly about.

"Hey! Come and get it! Woo! Up here, you long neck loggerhead. I bet Godzilla would eat you for breakfast!" Eric shouted.

Jacob thought he saw Eric's eyes widen three sizes larger before his friend pulled back and dove over a table behind him.

The elasmosaur's head shot through the window in a blink. The long neck carried it forward all the way to the overturned table Eric and others hid behind.

The event happened so fast it stunned Jacob into momentary paralysis.

The snake-ish head hit the table, and the people hiding behind it cried out in shock. Opening its mouth and unleashing a reptilian *hiss*, the elasmosaur's bloodstained teeth held meaty remnants of its earlier victims.

The creature's jaws bit the table. And with a quick shake of its head, tossed it to the side.

Eric and four other passengers were about to lose their lives.

"Over here!" Jacob didn't know where his sudden burst of bravery came from, but he realized doing nothing would sentence those people to death. He was already responsible for killing one human and didn't want to add to that burden—even if it cost him his life. "Come get me. I got your birthday cake with candles." He stepped forward, moving the burning bundle in front of him.

The flares' sparkles caught the elasmosaur's attention. It sensed an attack, and the neck defensively pulled its head back.

The sailor threw a bottle of hot sauce and hit the sea creature on the nose.

It opened its mouth again and hissed a warning. The gaping jaws were wide enough to stuff a whole hog down its throat.

Jacob didn't have a hog, but he did have a burning bundle of flares.

He tossed the flaming weapon like shooting a basketball, with two hands. Whereas Jacob usually lost in a friendly game of *HORSE*, his aim was true and sent the flares smack into the middle of the elasmosaur's throat.

The elasmosaur's jaws closed, and in an instant, it slammed its head upward on the ceiling. It hissed and gagged, flaying its head about.

Jacob took a hit to his left side and heard ribs crack. He rolled on the floor and put his hands over his head. There was nothing left to do. This had either been the most heroic thing he had ever done or the most stupid thing which might end his life.

"It's gone!" the sailor said. He ran to the window and watched. "It's thrashing in the water. I don't think it can spit out the flares. You're burning up its guts."

Eric came over to his side. "Hey, man. You okay?"

"Yeah," Jacob said and tried to push himself off the floor. "Ouch! Dude, I might have some broken ribs."

"It stopped moving! I think it's dead!" the sailor said and grinned from ear to ear.

Cheers of delight rose from the passengers.

"Look at that, dude. You're a hero!" Eric said as he gingerly helped Jacob to his feet.

Thank-yous and *accolades* inundated Jacob as he steadied to his feet. But all that attention became a white noise clouding his vision.

His mind's eye kept returning to the unnamed man who had risked his life for him earlier and paid the ultimate price.

Jacob had made a mistake so egregious that nothing he could do would absolve the sin.

"I don't even know his name," he said; his words lost in the barrage of excitement; his soul in a cage that he may never escape.

CHAPTER 14

Officer Charles Tidwell gripped tightly to the waistband of his rescuer's jeans as the dirt bike careened down Decauter street. The driver's jacket had *Ardis* embroidered on the back.

Less than a minute ago, Tidwell was about to die a horrible death by a deadly creature from time's past. It took the bravery of an outlaw who risked his life to save him.

He glanced behind and saw the other three dirt bikes make their escape, along with the two ATVs whose riders had unpinned Sergeant Darryl Ginyard from underneath the carriage and take him away before the allosaurus ate him alive.

Crossing Canal Street, Tidwell saw the main street had become a parking lot. Some cars were abandoned, and some not. He imagined the fear of those trapped inside a vehicle with no way to leave. It was hot enough where if the windows weren't rolled down, or the air conditioning running, that temperatures could rise high enough to kill the passengers.

Then, he discovered the source of the traffic jam. A stegosaurus a few blocks up the street clogged the intersection. It looked as big as a float on Mardi Gras day. In fact, the beast had been bombarded from above with long strands of colorful beads, that now hung from the spade-shaped boney plates lining its back. If the situation hadn't been so dire, Tidwell would have laughed.

He remembered that a stegosaurus had a spiked tail. A heavy weapon like that could do major damage to thin sheet metal. Hopefully, the stegosaurus wouldn't consider vehicles much of a threat. Now wasn't a good time to lay on the horn to voice traffic frustrations.

Canal Street came and went. Where they headed, Tidwell didn't know, and that made him uneasy. He didn't think he could convince the Bywater Boyz gang member to *entrust* his dirt bike to him for *emergency police business*.

A few beeps came from one of the ATVs behind them as they approached Poydras Street.

Engines wound down, and vehicles braked to a stop at the intersection.

The ATV carrying Sergeant Ginyard pulled up even with Tidwell's ride.

"I got a hold of the Chief," Ginyard said. "They're emptying the Louisiana National Guard and the Army National Guard in the Ninth Ward and sending them to the Superdome to set up base. All available police units are heading there to secure the area."

Ardis, the driver of Tidwell's bike, lifted the face shield on his helmet. "My boys are going there too."

"Really? Why?" the sergeant asked.

"Come on, man," Ardis said. "You know when the crap hits the fan the poor people run to the Superdome for safety. Heck, I spent a few days in that hot-box during hurricane Katrina."

"The dome's up the road. Time to get while the getting is good," Tidwell said.

"Let's go," Ginyard said.

Ardis dropped his visor and goosed the throttle. The front tire lifted off the ground after turning on Poydras Street. He was no fool, he knew right now he had a *get out of jail free card* for anything short of murder.

Poydras Street had almost no traffic. Parked cars sporadically lined the road as always.

A vehicle from out of nowhere darted across an intersection in front of them, and Ardis and the others hit their brakes.

Dodging one bullet, fate doubled down as a two-legged dinosaur popped up from around the corner. It was easily twenty feet tall and looked a lot different from the allosaurus who had attacked them earlier.

This dinosaur had a long neck and lizard-like head. An array of feathers ran from its crown, down its spine, and all the way to its thin and relatively short tail.

Another unique feature, it had oversized three-fingered claws—the claws measuring nearly three feet long!

Tidwell had found himself thrown forward when Ardis braked, and now he almost tumbled off the back as the Bywater Boyz hit the accelerators to flee.

One of the dirt bike riders caught a swooping claw from the therizinosaurs. The three spike-like claws penetrated his chest and poked all the way through his back. The bike continued forward without its rider and crashed into the side of a building.

Ardis slammed on the brakes, and the bike fishtailed and spun around so far the back tire bumped a New Orleans Public Works truck. "Darius!" he yelled and lifted his visor.

Darius' arms and head listed lifelessly, but his legs twitched uncontrollably.

Dismounting the dirt bike, Ardis left Tidwell on his own. He then lowered to one knee and reached to his ankle. Coming away with a handgun from his ankle holster, he raised it and fired.

Tidwell slid forward in the seat and prevented the bike from falling on its side. When he saw Ardis produce a handgun, he yelled, "Stop! He's gone. Get back over here. We need to leave."

The others had stopped and watched the horror show.

Ardis had a small caliber gun which could do little, if any, real damage. As evident by the therizinosaurs paying him no mind. Instead, it fixated on the skewered fresh meat.

Darius' skull cracked and crunched as the dinosaur's jaws crushed it like popcorn.

Tidwell saw the pain on Ardis' face and wished there was a way he could help him extract revenge for his buddy. Not only that, but this monster didn't need to prey on the innocent of New Orleans. It needed to be destroyed now.

As he looked around, Tidwell spotted a five-gallon propane bottle in the back of the maintenance truck. It was a long shot, but a YouTube video he'd watched on *improvised explosives* inspired his next move.

He stood the dirt bike on its stand and went for the propane tank. It had a regulator on a rubber hose connected to the valve. He sawed the hose off with his serrated pocket knife and ran by Ardis' side. "Put the gun down!"

The therizinosaurs placed Darius on the ground and put a foot on his leg while its jaws worked on pulling off his right arm.

Opening the valve, propane hissed out the cut hose.

Sergeant Ginyard excitedly yelled something Tidwell couldn't understand. Didn't matter. There was a chance they could take care of this threat here and now.

Tidwell ran forward and waited to get close enough before he reared back and unleashed the propane bottle like it was a bowling ball.

The bottle skidded along the street before coming to a stop when it hit the therizinosaurs' leg.

Again, the dinosaur was only interested in eating.

Running to Ardis, he held out his hand. "Let me have that."

"No, it's mine. I've got a concealed carry permit," Ardis said.

"I'll give it back," Tidwell said.

Reluctantly, Ardis complied.

The *heavier than air* propane formed a visible cloud growing around the therizinosaurs. Tidwell waited for the dinosaur to lift its nose as it noticed something strange before he squeezed off a carefully aimed round.

The first bullet missed. But the second found its target and penetrated the tank. The explosion nearly sent Tidwell to his knees.

A glorious fireball engulfed the dinosaur. It slammed into a nearby wall and looked burnt to a crisp and bloated like it had swollen and popped. The concussion from the explosion possibly turned its insides to jelly.

Tidwell felt the concussion too; like his head got run over by a log truck. He looked and saw the others rubbing their ears and heads. They weren't as close to the explosion as the dinosaur but still had suffered some effects.

Ardis removed his helmet and wiped his wet eyes with his fingers.

"I'm sorry about your friend," Tidwell said.

Shaking his head, he said, "He…was my cousin."

Giving the poor man a minute to grieve, Tidwell said in a soft, instructive voice, "We need to get over to the dome. We'll come back and get his remains as soon as this is over," he said and handed the pistol to Ardis.

"That was some creative thinking, officer," Ginyard said, giving a rare half-grin showing two of his gold teeth.

This was the only time Tidwell had seen the sergeant smile like that outside of a bar when Ginyard was talking to a woman and drinking a Heineken. "Thanks. Let's go to the dome."

*

The blocks passed quickly down Poydras Street as the Bywater Boyz' vehicles ate pavement. Tidwell spotted a few dinosaurs roaming the narrower side streets. The dirt bike moved too fast for him to get a good look at them. But from what he saw, none were attacking humans, and none were taller than an average man. This inspired a little hope because if all the dinosaurs had been the size of the allosaurus or the therizinosaurs, whatever defense the police could put together wouldn't be enough.

As they approached the dome, cars cluttered the surrounding streets. Taking sidewalks and other off-road passages put them near the entrance to the Mercedez Benz Superdome.

They came to a stop by a line of police cars. Beyond the blockade, Tidwell saw people coming in droves from a nearby interstate ramp. A small number of police officers patrolled the area amongst the crowd, urging them toward the Superdome.

Tidwell hopped off the back of the dirt bike and waved at Chief Kenny Gregoire.

Gregoire broke his attention away from another officer and returned a slight nod before continuing his conversation.

Sergeant Ginyard joined Tidwell as the Bywater Boyz shut down their vehicles.

Gunshots cut through the air followed by a woman's scream. More gunshots followed from multiple weapons.

"Let the good times roll," Ginyard said and looked around. "We need firepower, and we need it fast."

Two four-door Jeeps painted with the Bywater Boyz logo rolled up.

Ardis and his other three companions walked over to greet their fellow gang members.

Tidwell almost called out to Ardis to thank the man before going their separate ways, but Chief Gregoire approached to meet them.

"What have you two been doing to end up with that bunch?" the chief asked, his left cheek puffy with sunflower seeds.

"It's a long story," Ginyard said.

"I've been trying to bust them for over a year now," the chief said. "There're enough public safety violations stacked up to put them all away for twenty years."

"I hear you, Chief," Tidwell said. "We had a real bad incident go down in Jackson Square. Fact is, the Sarge and I wouldn't be here unless those gangbangers had saved us. The Sarge was trapped under a carriage, and I was just about to lose an arm wrestling match with a baby Godzilla when the Boyz showed up and got us out of there."

"Don't matter," Gregoire said. "We'll find a closet in the dome to shove them in until we can haul them to jail."

"Chief, they risked their lives to save ours," Ginyard said. "You know the code: If a criminal helps save a policeman's life, we don't press charges. If you violate that trust now, no one will ever help an officer again."

The chief spat out a few sunflower seed shells and chewed the kernels. "Okay, you win. But when this is over, and they tear up the roads on their off-road vehicles, they're on their own."

"Fair enough," Ginyard said.

"Chief—" Tidwell started.

The chief burst out, "What the hell?" He rushed past Ginyard and Tidwell over to the Bywater Boyz' Jeeps.

Tidwell turned and counted nine gang members hanging around their vehicles. Each one had an AK-47 and enough extra magazines to win a war in a small country.

"Have you guys lost your minds?" the chief said. "You can't go parading the streets of New Orleans with automatic weapons. That's stupid!"

"They're not automatic weapons," Ardis said.

"That don't matter," the chief said. "You hand those things over right now."

"We will not," Ardis said. "These guns were bought legally. None of our members have done anything that would prevent us owning these guns."

"But—" the chief said.

"But, nothing," Ardis said. "What? You see a bunch of black men with guns, and you automatically think we're a bunch of thugs? We might live life on the edge a little bit, but we're not criminals. You don't have to be *white* to be a patriot."

"But—" the chief started again.

"But nothing, *homie*," Ardis said. "New Orleans is my city. I'm fifth generation born from slaves who came from Africa. These are *my* people here. The dome is *my house* that I'm going to protect. That badge you wear doesn't give you the right to stop me from defending what is mine."

The chief's face turned red but receded to normal as Ardis spoke. The brewing inner turmoil contorted his face.

"Can't you just deputize them, or something?" Tidwell asked, trying to fill the silence.

After a deep breath, the chief said, "Okay." He turned his gaze and locked eyes with Ardis. "If any of you get out of line at any time, you will be shot on sight. The SWAT team is in position around the dome. I'll contact them and give them the details. If any of you are caught coming out of a business with merchandise, you won't have to worry about a trial."

"No worries here," Ardis said, obviously offended by the chief's assumption.

The chief continued to stare, but it did nothing to rattle Ardis' stance. Then, Gregoire turned and twisted a knob on his radio. As he walked off, he gave instructions to the SWAT team.

"That went better than I thought," Ginyard said.

"You guys want guns? We have two extras," Ardis said.

"Heck yeah!" Tidwell said.

One of the gang members pulled two AKs out of a Jeep and handed them to the policemen. Another member gave them four thirty-round magazines each.

"A Tommy Gun is much more my style," Ginyard said. "Not with those round magazines like the gangsters in the nineteen twenties used. I prefer the World War Two stick magazines."

"Ever shot an AK?" Ardis asked.

"Nope. But I have handled an AR-fifteen."

"You won't have any trouble using an AK," Ardis said. "See that lever on the side? That's the safety." He lifted the lever. "The safety is *on*. You have to lift it to put in a new magazine. Then, push it back down and cycle the slide."

Ginyard did as instructed.

"You're ready to go," Ardis said.

Tidwell pulled the slide on his gun and snapped a bullet in place. "One of the sweetest sounds you'll ever hear."

"Okay, men. Let's get out there and protect the citizens," Sergeant Ginyard said and led the way.

Just as Tidwell turned to follow, Ardis grabbed him by the shoulder.

"Uh...I may have stretched the truth a little. A few of the guys *might* be in trouble if caught with a gun," Ardis said in a low voice.

"They're good guys, right?" Tidwell asked.

"The best. They just made a few mistakes as kids."

"We can stretch the truth for the greater good, then. Remember, I'm a cop. I've stretched the truth for the greater good all of my career," Tidwell said and winked.

*

Tidwell patrolled in front of the dome's entrance ramps. A police van arrived with handguns and ammo. It felt natural having a weapon back on his side.

People still wandered from the interstate and over from the side streets. So far he hadn't seen any dinosaurs, but SWAT team members randomly fired at unknown dangers. He hoped one of Ardis' buddies didn't stray from the mission and the chief's warning come true.

If luck were on their side, the majority of the dinosaurs would be concentrated in the French Quarter and not the greater New Orleans area. He didn't have a radio, and none of the other officers on patrol he spoke to had any more understanding of the situation than he. Although, one officer said MSY had shut down to all incoming and outgoing traffic.

"What's up, Charlie?" a gruff voice said.

Tidwell looked up and saw Duane Mitchell and John Achord, two of his *podnuh's* from his hunting camp. They were dressed in camo and carrying high-power hunting rifles.

"What are you two doing here?" Tidwell asked and gave each one a quick handshake.

"Oh, we was at the huntin' camp and on the way back home," Duane said.

"Hunting camp? With those rifles? It's not deer season. You can only hunt squirrels this time of year, and you'd turn them to dust if you shot them with those guns."

Where John was from, there were two branches of Achord families in Livingston Parish. One branch was the *lying* Achords, and the other the *outlaw* Achords. "Charlie, you know where I come from the only *seasons* we have are salt and pepper," John said, identifying his heritage.

Officer Tidwell could only shake his head. "Boy, y'all are going to get the hunting camp lease revoked one day."

Duane smiled, his bottom lip swollen three times its normal size with Skoal. He picked a target on the street and spat. "After the traffic stopped on the interstate, we heard on the radio somethin' about pterodactyls at the airport, allosauruses at Antoine's, and brontosauruses on Bourbon Street. I thought that the radio DJ was pullin' our legs until I heard the same news on another station. They said we should find shelter and that the dome was takin' in refugees. Heck, we were less than a half a mile from here and hoofed it on over."

"Guys, you two have guns. Right now, the brass is looking the other way. You can keep yours, but be careful as *all-get-out* not to hurt or kill someone accidentally. Don't shoot at anything where you can't take a clear shot. I've seen dinosaurs. Some are as big as a turkey. Some are two stories tall," Tidwell said.

"I wonder what they taste like," John said. "If we kill a few, are they gonna let us take them home and eat them?" John may have been a poacher, but he always ate whatever he killed. He wasn't too proud to eat roadkill as long as it was still warm.

"John, that's not up to me," Tidwell said.

"Well if we kill something I might sneak a piece off and put it in the bucket," John said, bringing forward the red Arctic Swinger cooler in his left hand. "You want a ham sammich? I got a couple left."

"No, John. Thanks, but I'm good," Tidwell said. There was a chance those sandwiches were freshly made a few days ago and had been in the Swinger ever since. He never understood how John hadn't died from food poisoning by now.

"I think I see one!" Duane said. "Look!" He pointed to the sky.

A bat-like, flying reptile circled the Superdome.

"That thing's uglier than a turkey vulture," Duane said.

Tidwell agreed. The triangular shaped head of the pterodactyl looked devilish, and the wings made it look like a demon from out of Hell.

An AK-47 barked in the distance. One of the Bywater Boyz had an ostrich-like dinosaur in his sights and was shooting to bring it down.

Another gang member nearby him started shooting too.

The dinosaur stood almost ten feet tall and had a horny beak on a small head attached to a long neck. The long legs and tail made it look huge.

Seeing the ornithomimus reminded Tidwell of an encounter he had with an ostrich when he was just a small boy. He was at the zoo near a fence housing the big birds. His finger was inches away from the fence when he pointed for his mother to look. The ostrich stuck its beak through the diamond-patterned wire fence and bit his fingertip. Tidwell hated ostriches ever since that day. His anger stirred, he wished he could take a shot at the dinosaur but was afraid he'd hit innocent people.

The Bywater Boyz rattled off many shots, but the dinosaur kept its pace until its beak got within striking distance. The ornithomimus dropped its head like a battering ram.

Tidwell heard what sounded like a baseball hit out of the park.

The unfortunate gang member dropped to the ground as hard as a bag of rocks. A large gash in his skull spilled a river of blood.

By now the accumulation of hot lead in the ornithomimus took its toll. The dinosaur struggled to stand.

Taking advantage of the lull, the gang member stepped close enough to put the barrel of his rifle against the head of the ornithomimus and pulled the trigger.

It was the dinosaur's turn to die.

Before Tidwell could go to the fallen warrior's aid, members of the SWAT team began a barrage of fire.

Coming up Poydras Street, a mass of creatures rushed toward them. It reminded Tidwell of a herd of sheep. But these creatures were nothing like sheep.

What made matters worse, three people ran for their lives in front of the herd.

The approaching terror didn't go unnoticed by other officers or Bywater Boyz. They migrated to meet the oncoming threat.

SKEER-AK!

The pterodactyl took everyone unaware as it swooped down and caught a small woman heading up the entrance ramp to the dome. Its foot claws dug into her shoulders and gained altitude with each flap of its leathery wings.

The woman screamed, but everyone was helpless to save her. If anyone had shot, there was a chance she would get hit. And if they did shoot the flying reptile, then she would perish from the long fall to earth. The hopeless situation burned a hole in Tidwell's gut.

John had his elbow on a concrete rail and his eye on the scope of his Remington 7mm mag rifle. He squeezed off a round and giggled. "Got 'im." He giggled again and slid the bolt back to load the next bullet.

By this time Tidwell's strained eyes allowed him to see the oncoming dinosaurs' features. They also showed him that the three people in front were losing the race.

The slowest man smashed face-first onto the asphalt. Hungry two-legged dinosaurs as tall as calfs flocked to feed on his flesh. These dinosaurs resembled common green lizards except with their back legs and neck stretched. Of course, the mouths were large enough to fit around a human's head.

"Get out of the way! Get out of the way!" an officer cried and waved his arms, warning the two runners to move and clear a path for shooting.

One runner veered to the right, and the other slipped and fell.

Police and armed citizens unloaded their weapons on the approaching coelophyses.

Some dinosaurs stopped and fed on the second runner, but the others showed no fear—even as their members succumbed to flying lead.

Any gun discharge scared animals in the wild. Tidwell expected the noise alone would have been enough to send these dinosaurs scurrying. No such luck.

The rifles did a good job mowing down coelophyses, but as the herd thinned and the survivors neared, the battle became all too real.

The first coelophysis to reach an officer bit his arm as he struggled with the slide on his pistol. The poor man pummeled the dinosaur on its head with the handgun trying to get it to release its grinding jaws.

Tidwell rushed to his aid but had to deal with two coelophyses seeking to cut him off.

He brought the AK to his side and fired from the hip.

One dinosaur dropped, but the other was on top of him. All he had time to do was bring the rifle up with his two hands and use it to keep the creature at bay.

When the coelophysis reared back on its legs, its head came just above Tidwell's chin. It hissed, and vile breath assaulted his nostrils.

He managed to swing the stock and pound the beast on its left side—hoping to crack a few ribs.

It backed off a step and then lunged its head forward for the kill.

Bringing up the rifle, Tidwell caught it under the jaw, knocking spit from its mouth.

But the coelophysis was undeterred, lowering its head, and knocking the officer to the ground.

He barely had time to bring the rifle in position as the open jaws went for his throat. Instead of soft flesh that would fold like a toilet paper tube, the rows of nail-like teeth bit down on steel barrel and wood front stock.

Tidwell tried pushing the head back, but the dinosaur was too strong. His muscles tensed and burned. There was no way for him to overpower this prehistoric creature.

Then Tidwell saw John behind the dinosaur. Wearing a big grin on his face, the man shoved the rifle's barrel right under the coelophysis' tail.

The beast unlatched its jaws and spun around, standing high on its legs. It hissed and raised its arms at John.

John shook the rifle at the dinosaur. "You want some more of this?" He giggled, and said to Tidwell, "Shoot 'im—"

A quick double tap from his handgun put two bullets where Tidwell thought its heart should be. Not taking any chances, he then unloaded his pistol into its torso.

The coelophysis keeled over and died.

Lowering a hand, John helped the officer to his feet. "The head on that thing would look good mounted and hanging on your living room wall."

"Ah, I don't know. The girlfriend gets freaked out by animal trophies," Tidwell said.

"Get a new girlfriend," John said. The man always had a simple solution to the most difficult of problems.

The shooting stopped. Tidwell turned his gaze and saw all the dinosaurs were dead and counted four men, two of the Bywater Boyz and two police officers, who would not see the sunset in the afternoon.

BAM!

Duane had his rifle pointed to the sky and then lowered the barrel toward the ground. "WOO-WE! I shot *that* pterodactyl in the *EYYYE...BALL.*"

The winged reptile fell from the air and crashed onto the second level open parking lot on the east side of the Superdome.

The SWAT team fired again before Tidwell had a chance to catch his breath. When he looked down Poydras Street, he realized something for the first time.

Tyrannosauruses hunted in herds too.

The *tyrant lizards* were a few blocks away, and they made the coelophyses look like lap dogs.

"Boys, we are in a pile of trouble," Tidwell said.

A low hum sounded in the distance. At first, the officer wondered if the T. rex entourage made the earth shake. But, the noise grew louder, and in no time Tidwell knew exactly what it was.

"Gunship!" Tidwell said as the Apache helicopter flew overhead, straight toward the dinosaurs.

The helicopter unleashed a Hellfire rocket, and it hit its target in the blink of an eye. A dome of orange grew like the inside of the sun before black smoke rose into the sky.

One tyrannosaurus had escaped harm and ran for safety.

The Apache pursued and made hamburger of it with its 30mm cannon.

"There won't be anything left worth eating on the critter," John said. "That helicopter might be fun to hunt hogs out of."

Four Chinook helicopters flew in across the horizon and proceeded to hover above the Superdome.

Incoming people and those making their way up the ramp cheered and clapped.

Someone chanted, "USA! USA!" ; uniting the people as one.

Charles Tidwell felt a lump in his throat and tears swell in his eyes. The good guys had finally arrived.

The military would put a boot up those dinosaurs' asses. It was the American way.

THE DINOSAUR BATTLE OF NEW ORLEANS

CHAPTER 15

"What do you mean you like the idea of an all-white America?" Randy Guillaume asked of Doug, his nephew. "The Sons of the Confederacy recognize the rights of every race. We're not white supremacists. We may like keeping to our own kind, but blacks prefer their kind too."

"You crackers want to keep us *boys* in our place. The fact is, is that you will never treat us as equals until all symbols of racism are wiped away from every book, every street, and every name on every public building. The playing field must be equal. And outfits like your Sons of the Confederacy and National Socialist need to be eradicated too," Rev. Scott said, stepping into Randy's personal space.

"See, Uncle Randy. He wants to wipe us out. I say we get them before they get us. It just makes sense," Doug said.

Andrew Jackson watched the smoldering embers on each side catch fire. Rev. Scott wasn't going to give an inch.

The NSM member smirked watching Randy and Doug at odds, knowing he had just scored a convert.

Tim, Randy's other nephew, migrated from the storm and perched by a window.

"Guys, don't you realize that both sides of this argument are tearing our country apart?" Andrew said. "The American Republic was founded on the belief that all people are created equal. Fundamental rights, such as liberty, free speech, freedom of religion, and due process of law, are for everyone."

"Yeah? Tell that to the American Indians. The white man took all of that away," Rev. Scott said.

"Native Americans are citizens of their tribal nations as well as the United States. So, your point is not valid. And, you aren't championing the Native Americans' cause anyway."

"You're wrong. Native Americans recognize the atrocities of the white supremacists. You can sing Yankee Doodle Dandy all day long, but that's just keeping the boot on minorities' throats.

"If you preach a scorched-earth you will inherit a scorched-earth," Andrew said. "There has to be a way for you, the Sons of the Confederacy, and even the Alt-Left and Right to coexist. That is the only way for America to survive."

"If that's what it takes for America to survive, then I don't care if America burns to the ground. We can build a new America. One where all men and women can truly be equal," Rev. Scott said.

"See, he wants war," the NSM member said.

"Not if you back out of the way and do the right thing," Rev. Scott said.

"That will never happen," the NSM member said.

"And how many innocent people will die on both sides because neither will compromise?" Andrew asked.

"Only one side is innocent. Everyone on the other side is guilty and deserves to die," Rev. Scott said.

"I've had about enough of your mouth," Doug said. He reached out to grab Rev. Scott, but Randy seized his arms. Andrew stepped in front of the protest leader.

"Boy, your momma raised you better than that," Randy said.

"Get out of my way," Rev. Scott said to Andrew. "I don't need a white man to fight my battles." He then winced in pain and grabbed his hurt knee.

"You need to sit down and rest," Andrew said. Then, he said to all, "If we somehow make it out of here without killing each other, we can pick a time and a place to meet and *kill each other* later."

His outburst seemed to diffuse the situation for the moment.

Rev. Scott nursed his knee.

Doug jerked his arm from his uncle's grip.

The NSM member frowned like he had a bad taste in his mouth.

Tim continued to pretend he wasn't in the room to avoid conflict and gazed through the window.

*

Lieutenant Kevin 'Nuke' Tassin held his 9mm pistol with both hands up near his right shoulder as he warily entered the baggage gateway on the first floor of the airport. He had always wondered how the luggage got from the airplane to the conveyor belt and now had a bird's-eye view.

Something was definitely going on outside of baggage pickup.

Kevin hopped on the conveyor belt and dropped to his knees as he rode it past the cloth strips and into the baggage area.

Suitcases and carry-ons littered the floors. There were several dead bodies, three of whom wore TSA uniforms, and a few of the bird-reptile creatures like the one he had encountered before also dead.

At least the doors leading outside were closed and hopefully locked. A large shape moved past a window, but he didn't get a good enough look to tell what it was.

"Help!"

Kevin ran past the conveyor belt and saw near the escalator to concourses C and D, a TSA agent awkwardly poking a chair at a velociraptor.

Watching his footing, Kevin dashed to help the man before it was too late.

This dinosaur hadn't been knocked senseless from a fall like the one he'd killed earlier. It leaped and savagely slashed the bottom of the chair with the claws on its feet.

"I'm out of ammo. Watch out for those claws!" the TSA agent yelled.

The agent was in the line of fire, so Kevin didn't have a shot. He veered his path so that he could run even with it without getting too close.

But the velociraptor sensed him coming and stopped its assault, turning and hissing a warning.

Now Kevin was in the dinosaur's sights, and he couldn't fire his pistol without risking the TSA agent. *Who dat say who dat when I say who dat?*

Instead of running for cover, the TSA agent smashed the chair against the raptor's body.

The dinosaur hissed and stumbled, but then felt the full force of Kevin's 9mm.

Bullet after bullet tore into the dinosaur's torso. The shots didn't stop until the velociraptor went down for the count.

Kevin kept a bead on it as he approached it. When he was close enough, he gave it a swift kick to ensure it was dead.

"You okay?" Kevin asked, keeping his gaze on the creature.

"Yeah. I'm good," the man said. "Who are you?"

"Lieutenant Kevin Tassin. I'm from the Joint Reserve Base." He turned and saw the agent had a nametag that read CRAIS. "I was sent here to check on the pterodactyls that invaded the airspace. Long story short, I crashed my jet and ended up here."

"Crashed your jet? That must have been one of the explosions I heard," Crais said.

"Yeah. The other one was a fuel truck. That's a long story too."

Crais dropped his head. "I have no idea what's going on around here. One minute it's business as usual and then all hell breaks loose." He turned his gaze over to the dead bodies on the floor. "We lost some good men today."

"That's too bad," Kevin said, knowing what it's like to lose a teammate.

"I'm not sure how many of these creatures made it in here before we locked-down. I think most are dead, but a few made it up the stairs."

"I'm down to half a magazine and have one full spare. You said you were out of bullets?" Kevin asked.

"Yeah, and as much as I hate to, I will have to get some from…" the words caught in Crais' throat.

Kevin looked toward the fallen heroes. The thought of pilfering their ammo seemed so disrespectful.

"Hey, you two okay ?" a voice said from the top of the escalator.

"Darren!" Crais called out. "There are several people down. I don't think any are alive. How are things up there?"

"A few of those creatures made it to Concourse D. We had four casualties, but we're secure now as far as I know," Darren said.

Darren turned his head and yelled, "Over by the baggage pickup. You need to hurry."

An emergency team of six appeared and took the steps down to the next level.

Crais waved his hand as they hit the floor, and said, "We're okay! We're okay! Keep going."

"Crais, you look white as a ghost. Why don't both of you come up here and take a load off."

Crais turned his gaze to Kevin, who put his pistol in its holster, and said, "After you."

The two rode the escalator. Kevin had his hand on the small of Crais' back in fear the man's knees might buckle and fall.

The heavenly scent of southern fried chicken wafted in the air as Kevin neared the top.

Darren welcomed Crais and helped him over to a chair. He then told another TSA agent to get him a drink.

Looking around, the food court bustled with business. People stranded at the airport had to do something to fill the extra time on their hands. The famous Dooky Chase's offered genuine soul food guaranteed to satisfy the hardiest of appetites. He couldn't believe after all he'd just been through, his stomach rumbled reminding him it was empty.

Seeing that Crais was well taken care of, he headed toward the restaurant.

Before he made it halfway there, someone yelled, "Where y'at!"

He turned his gaze and saw two men sitting at a table having beers in front of a bar. One man had a shining black eye and looked familiar.

"Tassin the *assassin*!" Ritchie Lemonie said; assassin the nickname Kevin earned on the football field.

"Ritchie!" Kevin hurried over to shake hands.

"Man, I wondered if you were okay. We saw your parachute after the jet crashed," Ritchie said.

"I wondered what happened in the control tower. Those pterodactyls fell out of the sky like rocks," Kevin said.

"We lost one teammate," Ritchie said. "A pterodactyl smashed through the window and killed him instantly. Mark," he tilted his head toward his fellow air traffic controller, "and the rest of us made it out alive."

"Hi, Kevin. I'm the controller you spoke with earlier. Hook you up with a beer?" Mark said and spat into an empty cup.

"Sure, hook me up." Kevin took a seat in an empty chair.

Mark caught the attention of a server, and said, "Three more."

"This whole situation is crazy," Kevin said. "How is it possible for dinosaurs extinct for millions of years to just pop up from out of nowhere? One thing I'm curious about is how widespread is this going on?"

"From what little we've been told, the phenomena hasn't been reported outside of New Orleans. People are posting YouTube videos, and the whole nation knows what's happening. The president's already declared an emergency, and the military and police are moving as fast as they can. Everyone is ordered to stay in place."

The server set three fresh beers on the table.

Kevin brought his beer up with the two others and clinked mugs. After a taste, he said, "Like mother's milk." He followed the taste with a chug. "Hey Ritchie, that's a nasty looking black eye you have there. Dinosaur land a haymaker on you?"

Ritchie's face went blank for a moment. He turned and looked at Mark.

"He fell and hit a door," Mark said and spat into a cup.

Turning his gaze back to Kevin, Ritchie said, "I fell and hit a door."

Uncomfortable silence rolled over the table for several moments.

"It's all good now," Mark said, and then loaded his bottom lip with a fresh dip.

*

Broderick Brown had one hand on the streetcar's brake as he sat awkwardly in the seat. He had switched the control of the vehicle's motion so he could pilot it in reverse.

Dionne, his wife, and Keesha, his daughter, sat snugly together on a front seat, hunched over and with arms crossed over their chests.

T-Bob, the zoo employee who had risked his life multiple times to help Broderick's family, knelt on a seat in the front and kept watch for sudden dangers.

The streetcar rail ran on the levee, with the Mississippi River to one side and a block or so deep of wooded area on the other side.

So far he had seen five different types of dinosaurs eating from tree leaves. Three were of the two-legged variety, and two had four legs. None seemed interested in pursuing the streetcar. He was certain Keesha could identify them, but this was no time for games.

Poor Keesha! The little girl had been through so much in such a short amount of time. What was she dealing with internally?

Dionne looked broken. A wave of guilt washed over Broderick as he had seen that same expression several times over the years; after their proverbial *knock-down, drag-out* arguments. He saw for the first time the depths of the damage he had done to the woman who was supposed to be the love of his life. By failing his wife, he had undoubtedly failed his daughter. Was there really any way to repair what he had destroyed?

"We're about to lose the trees. Coming up on Mardi Gras World," T-Bob said.

Mardi Gras World was a 300,000 square foot working warehouse where large floats were made for Mardi Gras parades in New Orleans. Tourists also visited to get an up-close view of the magnificent creations.

Broderick considered stopping the streetcar and taking refuge there, but then saw several dinosaurs lurking in front of the warehouse.

The convention center was right next door. The parking lot had their share of prehistoric creatures too.

By this time Broderick figured everyone had sheltered in place. Roaming the streets was suicide, and yet he and his family were riding in a tin can that didn't protect the earlier riders. He wanted four walls and a roof in the worst sort of way.

They were about to go under the interstate. Traffic had come to a standstill. He didn't envy that situation at all.

Vehicles clogged Canal Street as they passed. They were only a few blocks away from their destination. Everything felt surreal. This area by the river normally teemed with people, but there were none. Zero. There weren't any dinosaurs either. That was encouraging, but he knew not to let his guard down.

"We're still going to the cathedral?" T-Bob asked.

"Yeah. We're getting close," Brodrick said. He adjusted the accelerator to begin a smooth stop.

"Dionne, Keesha, get ready. The cathedral is only about three blocks from the river. We need to stay together and move as fast as possible."

Dionne looked up, bit her lip, and nodded.

"Keesha, Poppy is waiting for us. You know where the cathedral is. We're all going to stay together. *But*, if anything happens…if for some reason something bad happens, you need to run away as fast as you can to the cathedral. Don't worry about mommy and daddy. Don't look back. Keep your eyes on those doors and run. Can you do that for me?"

Keesha shifted her gaze to the side. A tear rolled down her right cheek. "I understand, Daddy."

"Coming up on the park," T-Bob said.

Broderick slowed the streetcar and brought it to a stop. There still wasn't a soul to be seen—human or dinosaur. This was no time for second thoughts. It was do or die, or do *and* die. The thought hit him in the gut so hard he thought he might puke.

He had to push through, though. "Let's go."

Broderick opened the door and went down the steps onto the pavement. He had his pistol in his hand and looked around. "All clear."

Dionne stepped out with Keesha in tow.

T-Bob popped out next.

"I'm taking the lead," Broderick said. "T-Bob, take the rear."

"Got it," T-Bob said.

After filling his lungs with fresh air, Broderick trotted down the walkway leading to the Washington Artillery Park memorial. His head on a swivel, he kept shifting his gaze to the front and sides, with an occasional glance behind to see Keesha just a step or two away and Dionne hovering over her.

T-Bob's expression showed his determination to stick this thing through to the bitter end, no matter what the consequences.

They came to the wall where a set of stairs to the left and right led to the top of the memorial. He turned left and climbed quickly to the top, intending to reach the open area well before the others.

No one in sight. The park benches were empty, and the ancient artillery cannon in the center of the tiled deck free of the usual tourists.

"Still good," he said and moved to allow the rest onto the deck.

St. Louis Cathedral laid directly in front of them; separated by Decauter Street and Jackson Square. As he stepped cautiously forward, the battlefield came into view.

There were parts of dead bodies and bloodstains on the street. Abandoned cars and an overturned horse carriage remained as casualties.

Then, it hit him. The statue of Andrew Jackson that stood proudly for decades in front of the cathedral was no longer there!

"Is it safe to go down?" Dionne asked.

"I don't know," Broderick said. "I don't see any reason why we shouldn't make a run for it. We can't just stay up here." There was the fear that if good fortune had given them a window, they would lose it if they delayed any longer.

"T-Bob?" Broderick said.

"You have a plan. We have to stick to the plan unless there is a reason not to," T-Bob said.

It was the simplest of conclusions but unarguable.

"We just have to cross the street and the park. We're going to run as fast as we can once we get down the stairs," Broderick said. "Stay close."

The first set of stairs had ten steps. That led to a flat walkway that turned into more steps. They hurried down, with Keesha stumbling once and kept from falling by her mother until they reached the street.

Looking around, Broderick was amazed that they were all alone. It was as if the angels protecting St. Louis Cathedral had extended their arms over the whole area.

"Stay away from the dead bodies," Broderick said, knowing there was no way of shielding his daughter from the carnage.

The four crossed the street and entered the gates of Jackson Park. There were dead members of the Sons of the Confederacy and the Alt-Right and Alt-Left. There were dead dinosaurs too. What Broderick didn't know, was if any of protestors had killed each other.

As they neared the middle of the park, Broderick saw the remains of Jackson's statue. It looked like it had been toppled over and broken into large chunks. *Poppy got his wish*, he thought.

As he led the four past the broken statue, his insides twisted when a dinosaur concealed behind the statue's base roared.

The dinosaur was twice the size of a grown man. It stood on two legs and had feathers on its arms and tail. The long mouth and sharp teeth looked deadly, but it was its long claws that Broderick feared the most.

There was no way his gun could take that thing down. He, his family, and T-Bob would die if they tried to outrun it.

There was only one thing to do.

He would rush the dinosaur and engage it, hopefully giving the rest enough time to make it to the cathedral.

Broderick pointed, and shouted, "Get to the cathedral! Now!"

There was no time to explain. There was no time to say goodbye and tell Dionne and Keesha how much he loved them and how sorry he was for not being there for them in the past.

The Utahraptor lowered its head and began its attack.

Broderick sprang forward and fired a shot after a few steps. Anything he could do to delay the monster a few seconds might be enough to save his family—even if it meant giving up his flesh for food.

The next thing Broderick knew, his back foot was kicked out from underneath him, and he rolled onto the ground.

T-Bob sped past, and shouted, "Go with your family! They need you!"

"No!" Broderick yelled, but then saw there was no turning the man back.

The Utahraptor welcomed T-Bob with sharp claws and an open mouth.

Not having the stomach or time to watch, Broderick took his gift and ran after his family.

Dionne and Keesha were in the middle of Chartres Street when he exited the gates of Jackson Park and passed the road construction fence.

They arrived at the double doors of St. Louis Cathedral together.

The doors opened, and they stepped inside.

CHAPTER 16

Andrew watched Rev. Scott massage his knee, and positioned himself between Doug and the NSM member, in case they tried to take a cheap shot at the protest leader.

Rev. Scott wasn't in any condition to defend himself, and the NSM member looked at him like a vulture waiting for a crippled animal to die.

He welcomed the silence of the last several minutes, but he was out of ideas on how to escape. They would have to wait for the police or military to make a sweep before they could leave. He hoped emotions wouldn't boil over and cause irreparable damage.

"A kid and a woman are coming this way," Tim said as he looked out the window.

Rev. Scott rolled onto his side and tried to stand.

"A man is behind them," Tim said. "They're heading straight for the cathedral." He turned to Randy as if he were waiting for instructions.

Andrew hurried to the door and opened it in time to receive the refugees.

A young girl ran in, with a thirty-something-year-old woman and man following.

"Keesha! Dionne!" Rev. Scott said in excited relief. He had somehow made it to his feet and balanced on his good leg.

"Poppy!" Keesha cried and ran to Rev. Scott's open arms.

The protest leader hugged his granddaughter and turned glistening eyes at Dionne. "Are you okay, baby?"

"We're fine, Daddy," she said between breaths. "We're fine."

"He's got a gun!" Doug said when the man entered; as if the weapon was a cobra about to strike.

"Broderick! Don't give up your gun!" Rev. Scott yelled.

Broderick brought the gun to his side and put his left hand over his face. He slowly shook his head, and whispered, "T-Bob…"

Dionne reached over and patted Broderick on the shoulder. "I know, honey. I know." She hugged him.

Rev. Scott moved Keesha behind him. "You came at the right time. These white men were looking for a place to hang me from."

Broderick turned his gaze over toward Rev. Scott. "Martin? What are you talking about?"

"Look at them. Three Johnny Rebs and a goose-stepping socialist. They were discussing how better off the world would be if I weren't around anymore."

"Rev. Scott, you're exaggerating things," Andrew said.

"Who are you with?" Broderick asked.

"Mommy!" Keesha said, looking out a window.

"Not now, Keesha," Dionne said.

"My name is Andrew R. Jackson. I was at the protest today to help save the statue. And, I'm not a member of any group. I am a descendant of General Jackson, and I support the preservation of history."

Broderick brought the pistol up near his chest but didn't point it at anyone.

"Give me the gun, Broderick," Rev. Scott demanded. "I'm the one in danger. They want the leader, not you."

"But Mommy, there's a puppy outside," Keesha said.

"*Not now*, Keesha," Dionne said, her voice heating up like the situation.

"It's my gun," Broderick said. "And I'm keeping it."

Rev. Scott hopped and stumbled forward as he tried to snatch the gun from Broderick's hand.

"Daddy!" Dionne screamed as she was knocked off balance and fell to the floor.

Doug rushed to the fray, pushing Andrew aside.

"Douglas!" Randy snapped and went after him. "Get off of him, boy!"

"Stop! All of you!" Andrew yelled.

Keesha ran from her spot by the window. At first, Andrew thought she was trying to get out of the way as the people wrestled on the floor. But then the little girl opened the door and ran outside.

That was the last thing Andrew expected.

He headed for the door where the NSM member stepped up to block him. "Let her go."

Shoving the socialist aside, he bounded out the door and saw Keesha running toward a small dog. "Keesha, come back!"

There was no turning her, though. Keesha only focused on the dog. She didn't see the Utahraptor prowling the premises.

The dinosaur hissed as it advanced to attack.

Keesha picked up the dog and froze when she saw it.

"Run, Keesha! Run!" Andrew yelled as he dashed up to the plastic fenced-off area on the street. Spotting several pieces of rebar for the road repair, he grabbed a length, placing his left hand on the bottom side and his right hand on the top side—holding the thick, rusty rod like a spear.

Dionne call for Keesha, and the little girl broke from her enchantment and ran toward the cathedral.

The Utahraptor was almost on top of them both.

"Run, Keesha! Run!" Andrew screamed again as she passed and the dinosaur powered toward him.

The Utahraptor's mouth opened, showing all of its sharp teeth.

A fan of history, Andrew remembered a tactic used by gladiators when they faced wild beasts in the Coliseum. Use the weight of the beast against itself.

He skidded to a halt and planted the butt end of the rebar in a joint between brick pavers. Then, he lowered the front end to meet the Utahraptor chest level.

The dinosaur hit the rebar and shrieked in surprise.

Andrew struggled to hold the steel rod in place as it penetrated the dinosaur's chest. His plan had worked! But the momentum of the beast that skewered it, also brought it closer.

The Utahraptor swiped one of its deadly claws and slashed him across the neck.

Andrew hit the ground as the world spun around in his head. His neck burned like fire, but then a cooling sensation followed. He put his hand on the wound and felt blood gushing from his jugular.

Even if EMTs were on the spot, there would be no saving him.

The Utahraptor had slumped on its side; the rebar had found its heart and killed it.

He looked over at the cathedral.

Broderick and Dionne stood at the door. He saw Keesha holding the dog between them.

Andrew then turned his gaze toward the three spires of St. Louis Cathedral. He was about to die, and this was the last place he would have imagined. Dying here, though, would be a privilege. It certainly was better than leaving this life from inside a cold, sterile hospital room.

Feeling lightheaded, soothing, angelic music grew in volume in the distance bringing him comfort. Andrew felt time's pull of gravity slowly lose its grip.

The weight of all his worldly burdens melted, freeing his spirit from the chains of its mortal coil.

Andrew heard his name called from the heavens. He closed his eyes. The corners of his mouth widened, and he followed the voice home.

EPILOGUE

The New Orleans Times

The Dinosaur Battle of New Orleans: One Year Later

By Norbert Reaux

This day marks one year since dinosaurs invaded the historic city of New Orleans. Though no authority has come forth with an explanation of what propelled the prehistoric creatures into modern times, the event is believed to have links to a secret NASA project once housed at Tulane University.

The time-shift anomaly forced ordinary citizens and tourists to defend themselves as the French Quarter, and surrounding areas, plunged into chaos. In all, over a thousand people perished; including police, firemen, EMTs, and military personnel.

A memorial service will be held at Jackson Square at noon today. The mayor Mitch Edwards, along with Tear Them to the Ground activist leader, Rev. Martin Scott, will be present to perform the service.

Rev. Martin Scott will also have the honor to unveil the replacement of the famous equestrian statue commemorating General Andrew Jackson's victory over the British during the War of 1812, destroyed by a giganotosaurus on that fateful day.

The mayor will present General Pete Hilderbrand the Key to the City for his strategic success in reclaiming the city block by block, and herding the dinosaurs to the Chalmette Battlefield. Corralling the prehistoric beasts to an open area, light armor and attack helicopters ended the threat, saving millions of dollars in collateral damage.

Bonnie the brontosaurus, one of the few surviving dinosaurs of the onslaught, will have her new home opened to the public at the Audubon Zoo next month. >see Battle, page 4A

*

Horns blew, and drums pounded in the jazz band. New Orleanians' even celebrated the solemn events in the Big Easy. *Cry at birth and laugh at death*, was an old African proverb.

At a jazz funeral, once the cortège left the cemetery, the wails of grief, intended to help the soul relieve its burdens, transformed into cries of joy, to assist the soul to dance their way into Heaven.

Laissez Les Bon Temps Rouler.

Let the good times roll.

Jackson Square bustled with energy as people vied for a spot near the center for the unveiling of the new statue.

On the stage set to one side of the covered monument, Mayor Edwards read the last name of the final casualty of the Dinosaur Battle of New Orleans, and the Rev. Martin Scott rang a bell to end the ceremony.

Edwards took a seat, and Rev. Scott stepped behind the podium.

The Reverend closed his eyes and turned his face to the sky, with a smile and a nod, he said, "I have the great honor to pay homage to one of the worst tragedies in modern history. And though my heart is heavy with the pain of losing so many loved ones a year ago today, I am inspired by the diverse individuals who have joined in the spirit of unity that stand before me."

Spreading his hands to either side, he said, "I look out and see members of Tear Them to the Ground, the Sons of the Confederacy, the Alt-Left, and the Alt-Right. It warms my heart that they are not raising arms against each other. Even though their positions could not be further apart. This simply proves there is a greater good that lives inside every human. A part of God, if you will, unstained by the trials of life. Today is proof that all of mankind can have differences of opinion and yet *still* share *one* like mind.

"The events of a year ago brought us here this day. But imagine leaving and going home and still share that like mind. Impossible, you say? Not long ago, I would have agreed with that.

"But I learned a valuable lesson a year ago. A lesson taught to me by a stranger. By a man who I viewed as an enemy.

"I came to realize the injustice perpetrated on me, and my race, created a cloud of bitterness that obscured my vision.

"Andrew Reagan Jackson was at the protest with me where one of the first dinosaur attacks took place. I sustained an injury during the turmoil, and he helped me out of Jackson Park, where we sought refuge in St. Louis Cathedral. One act of kindness from a white man did nothing to erase the scars of prejudice I've suffered over the last sixty years.

"But the scales fell from my eyes when Andrew, leaving the protection of the cathedral, gave his life to save my granddaughter, Keesha Brown.

"Minutes after Andrew perished, I held my granddaughter in my arms and felt fear unlike any other time in my life. I had been so close to losing her..." Rev. Scott paused as his voice broke.

He cleared his throat, and continued, "Keesha was alive. A great joy replaced the fear I had. My granddaughter was alive!" He raised his hands. "Hallelujah!"

Muffled affirmations rose from the audience.

Looking over the crowd, he said, "My granddaughter was alive, and she was saved...by a *white* man."

He let his last words hang in the air for a moment.

"A white man. Andrew R. Jackson. Then, I thought, *why would a white man give up his life for a black girl who he had no ties to*?

"I realized that it was because Andrew was a *man* first, and *white* second. This made me see too that I am a man first, and black, second.

"As men and women, we must first see all of humanity as equals—bound by an unyielding commitment of respect. We can have our differences, but we must never cross a line that fosters hate.

"Ladies and gentleman, I have not abandoned my cause. I realize the representatives from the various groups here still cling solidly to their beliefs.

"There is a test that will show if you are on the right or wrong path. If love and compassion for the advancement of all of mankind is not the center-point of your message, well, consider this: maybe you are preaching the *wrong* message.

"What I have learned, is that it is useless to force my will on others. It creates anger, dissent, and violence. I will instead continue my mission using love and enthusiasm—trying to win the hearts of my brothers and sisters—not create a void for us both to fall into.

"For those who reject my cause, I will stand by their side with an open hand of friendship. I will shine with the brightness of my message and drench them in love until they see the greater good.

"If I am by troubled waters and a person of hate falls into it, I will reach out and save them. Why, because as long as their heart still beats, I have time to win them over to my side.

"In time, if we all work together, I believe we will see the horrible scars of division melt away. Little by little, all people throughout America will join and be of like mind.

"My friends...and I do want everyone here today to always think of me as a friend, let us start the mission together, today."

Rev. Martin Scott nodded and pointed to a crane operator, who readied to lift the cover off the new statue.

The canvas tent slowly rose, revealing the new sentinel of Jackson Square.

Claps, cheers, and the full ensemble of a jazz band welcomed the commemoration of Andrew R. Jackson's sacrifice in the Dinosaur Battle of New Orleans.

The twenty thousand pound mass of metal depicted the heroic Jackson holding a length of rebar and stabbing an attacking Utahraptor in the chest. A bronze plate immortalized one of Andrew's known quotes:

History marks the path of triumphs and tragedies that instruct us how to unite and not divide.

Rev. Martin Scott raised his hands to quiet the crowd. "I am pleased to say, Jackson Square to this day and forever, will always be known, as *Jackson Square!*"

*

The muddy waters of the Mississippi River flowed down to the delta leading into the Gulf of Mexico.

Liopleurodons, elasmosaurs, plesiosaurs, giant squids, mosasaurs, and a host of other prehistoric dinosaurs and reptiles sought the vast oceans, looking for a new home and food to satisfy their insatiable appetites.

Many had eggs to lay.

All wanted to reign supreme in their new world.

THE END

CHECK OUT OTHER GREAT DINOSAUR THRILLERS

SPINOSAURUS
by Hugo Navikov

Brett Russell is a hunter of the rarest game. His targets are cryptids, animals denied by science. But they are well known by those living on the edges of civilization, where monsters attack and devour their animals and children and lay ruin to their shantytowns.
When a shadowy organization sends Brett to the Congo in search of the legendary dinosaur cryptid Kasai Rex, he will face much more than a terrifying monster from the past.
Spinosaurus is a dinosaur thriller packed with intrigue, action and giant prehistoric predators.

LAND OF DEATH
by Eric S Brown & Alex Laybourne

A group of American soldiers, fleeing an organized attack on their base camp in the Middle East, encounter a storm unlike anything they've seen before. When the storm subsides, they wake up to find themselves no longer in the desert and perhaps not even on Earth. The jungle they've been deposited in is a place ruled by prehistoric creatures long extinct. Each day is a struggle to survive as their ammo begins to run low and virtually everything they encounter, in this land they've been hurled into, is a deadly threat.

CHECK OUT OTHER GREAT DINOSAUR THRILLERS

JURASSIC ISLAND
by Viktor Zarkov

Guided by satellite photos and modern technology a ragtag group of survivalists and scientists travel to an uncharted island in the remote South Indian Ocean. Things go to hell in a hurry once the team reaches the island and the massive megalodon that attacked their boats is only the beginning of their desperate fight for survival.

Nothing could have prepared billionaire explorer Joseph Thornton and washed up archaeologist Christopher "Colt" McKinnon for the terrifying prehistoric creatures that wait for them on JURASSIC ISLAND!

K-REX
by L.Z. Hunter

Deep within the Congo jungle, Circuitz Mining employs mercenaries as security for its Coltan mining site. Armed with assault rifles and decades of experience, nothing should go wrong. However, the dangers within the jungle stretch beyond venomous snakes and poisonous spiders. There is more to fear than guerrillas and vicious animals. Undetected, something lurks under the expansive treetop canopy . . .

Something ancient.

Something dangerous.

Kasai Rex!

CHECK OUT OTHER GREAT DINOSAUR THRILLERS

WRITTEN IN STONE
by David Rhodes

Charles Dawson is trapped 100 million years in the past. Trying to survive from day to day in a world of dinosaurs he devises a plan to change his fate. As he begins to write messages in the soft mud of a nearby stream, he can only hope they will be found by someone who can stop his time travel. Professor Ron Fontana and Professor Ray Taggit, scientists with opposing views, each discover the fossilized messages. While attempting to save Charles, Professor Fontana, his daughter Lauren and their friend Danny are forced to join Taggit and his group of mercenaries. Taggit does not intend to rescue Charles Dawson, but to force Dawson to travel back in time to gather samples for Taggit's fame and fortune. As the two groups jump through time they find they must work together to make it back alive as this fast-paced thriller climaxes at the very moment the age of dinosaurs is ending.

HARD TIME
by Alex Laybourne

Rookie officer Peter Malone and his heavily armed team are sent on a deadly mission to extract a dangerous criminal from a classified prison world. A Kruger Correctional facility where only the hardest, most vicious criminals are sent to fend for themselves, never to return.

But when the team come face to face with ancient beasts from a lost world, their mission is changed. The new objective: Survive.

www.ingramcontent.com/pod-product-compliance
Lightning Source LLC
Chambersburg PA
CBHW032011170626
46807CB00006B/2755